LUCIE

Amalie Skram

Some other books from Norvik Press

LUCIE

Amalie Skram

Translated by
Katherine Hanson
and
Judith Messick

Norvik Press
2001

Originally published in Norwegian under the title of *Lucie* (1888).

This translation © 2001 Katherine Hanson and Judith Messick.

The Translators assert their moral right to be identified as the Translators of the work in relation to all such rights as are granted by the Translators to the publisher under the terms and conditions of their Agreement.

A catalogue record for this book is available from the British Library.
ISBN 1 870041 48 8
First published 2001

Norvik Press gratefully acknowledges the financial assistance given by NORLA (Norwegian Literature Abroad) for the translation of this book.

Norvik Press was established in 1984 with financial support from the University of East Anglia, the Danish Ministry for Cultural Affairs, the Norwegian Cultural Department and the Swedish Institute.

Managing Editors: Janet Garton and Michael Robinson.

Printed in Great Britain by Page Bros. (Norwich) Ltd, Norwich, UK.

I
In the Professors' Quarter

'Let's see how it looks on me.' Lucie seized a black tulle hat with yellow flowers from the chair where Nilsen had placed it, and put it on as she walked over to the mirror between the windows.

Nilsen, a lanky, aging spinster with a faded complexion and a wide Grecian nose, was wearing a shabby black alpaca dress, the skirt pinned up, its pleating wrinkled at the hem. Her hair was a tangled mass of rolls and braids that looked like hemp. Her wide mouth had a thick, fleshy lower lip with no trace of a curve and an upper lip that was no more than a narrow line.

'Citchy Coo!' cried Nilsen, tickling Lucie under the chin. 'I should be the one! I'd be Mrs. Gerner in no time, I'd see to that.'

Lucie skipped away from the mirror with a playful laugh and put the hat down.

'Just look at all he does for you, Luciekins!' Nilsen glanced around the rectangular room at the brown upholstered furniture whose pale wood proclaimed that they were new, and peered into the open door of the bedroom. 'Every time I come here you've got something new. That fancy cabinet with the brass plates and knickknacks, and this easy chair – you didn't have them the last time – and those pictures on the wall.'

'They don't amount to much,' Lucie said with a quick glance at some lithographs in dark lacquered frames.

'Not on these long walls! If I didn't love you so much, I'd be jealous, I really would.' As she spoke, Nilsen stuck out her thick wet tongue under her false upper teeth and cocked her head. She sounded like a child who still couldn't talk properly.

5

'Really, jealous of this,' Lucie said, arching her delicate eyebrows.

'He's going to marry you, by God! Shall we make a bet?' Nilsen reached out and wagged her index finger in front of Lucie's face. 'If you're smart and play your cards right. Shall we make a bet? But then you'll have to give me something pretty if you win.'

'Oh, go on!' Lucie said, swatting the hand away with a reluctant smile.

'And all the fine clothes he buys you,' Nilsen went on. 'Lord, how that heavy yellow lace dresses up that blue fabric.' She looked admiringly at Lucie's smart linen dress. 'He's crazy in love with you, Luciekins, just like Olsen and me and all the rest. Oh, you can imagine Olsen – sitting around all dried up and sallow, sawing away on his violin. Anybody even mentions your name, and he turns as black as a thundercloud. Yes, by God. Lord help you Lucie.' She roared with laughter.

'It must be a guilty conscience. He didn't treat me very well, I'll tell you that – and maybe you think he was faithful to me?'

'Faithful!' cried Nilsen, jerking her head toward Lucie and exposing her thin, dark neck. 'Have you ever heard of a man who was faithful? No, once you've been around a little…' Her hands in constant motion, like the paws of a swimming dog, she recounted at great speed her romantic history from the time she was a young actress in Bergen with many suitors, until the present, when she lived by making hats and accessories for the cast at Tivoli, with free tickets to performances and unhindered access backstage. Lucie had heard it at least twenty times before.

'And after you're married, *I'll* get married, too,' Nilsen finished up, clapping her hands together. Her grey cheeks grew pink and her eyes blinked rapidly. 'Yes, by God! I'll get married – get married and become a rich, fine lady – and then I'll take my wedding trip, Lucie!' She launched into a dance – up and down the room she went, in her old thin shoes with worn-down heels and toes scuffed white, repeating the same thing again and again.

'Ha,ha,ha!' Lucie laughed, flinging herself down on an American wicker chair. 'Well, I've never seen anybody carry on like you do.'

'Then you'll see, I'll make a new start,' Nilsen continued. 'I'm no beauty, but I *do have* a nose. You have a tragic profile, Nilsen, the director told me. Turn your side to the audience and lift your head proudly when you refuse his offer.' She threw back her head, crossed her arms over her breast and declaimed, with her profile toward Lucie:

> That is no offer for me, Sir Knight!
> I may be poor and from humble stock,
> But my soul is as noble as yours,
> And a thousand times more pure.

'I always got applause for those lines – Bergen applause, you know, not the pitter-patter you get in this part of the country.' Her dull eyes had taken on a sparkling life, the large fleshy nostrils flared, and she made a smacking sound with her thick lower lip.

'Has somebody proposed to you?' Lucie asked.

'Is there ever a time when someone isn't proposing,' Nilsen laughed. 'But just not the right one. Just guess: Mercury!'

'Errand-Christiansen!' Lucie sat up in the chair with a start. '*He's* proposed to you! No, really?'

'Yes, what do you think about that! He must have taken leave of his senses. This is the third letter he's slipped into my hand. I've been ashamed to talk about it, yes, by God!' Nilsen pulled a folded note with no envelope out of her pocket and handed it to Lucie. 'Read it and you'll see.'

'I'll tell you something, Nilsen. Why not accept him? Such a nice kind old man. You'd see that he'd treat you very well and he's not all that poor either.'

'Accept him – me? Now really, Lucie old girl, I think I'm worth more than that. Yes, by God!' Nilsen looked offended.

'Good Lord, if the fellow is that crazy about you.'

'This is what you get from your friends! Friends, who ought to have your interests at heart. Well what can you expect from people with no refinement.' Nilsen's voice quivered, and with trembling hands she put on her hat.

'You're not really angry, are you?' Lucie had finished reading the letter and laid it aside. 'I didn't mean anything by it, you know. – My dear, you're not really angry?'

'Oh no, of course I'm not angry! I'm used to this kind of thing.' Nilsen threw on a black crocheted shawl that was full of holes from run stitches, fastened the ends together across her chest, and nodded her tragic profile: 'When you mix with people who don't understand you, this is what you get.' She grabbed her cotton parasol, said a curt farewell and hurried out.

Lucie laughed. It wouldn't be long before she'd come rushing in again. 'Good day, Luciekins.' Ugh. That hideous Bergen squawk of hers.

'Tralalalalalalalalala,' she danced some polka steps across the floor, into the bedroom, and stopped by the window to look at St. Hanshaugen, jutting up like a fortress with a flag on top, the contours sharp in the clear blue summer sky. It was so beautiful in the afternoon when the sun was gone. And those comical doves out there, flying from the dovecote to the ground and up to the ledge outside the kitchen window, the male in hot pursuit.

'Tralalalalalalalalala,' back across the floor into the sitting room. Her hands were pressed to her powerful hips, thumbs on her slim waist, her straight back arched so that her firm, high breasts jutted out.

'Tralalalalalalalalala' back and forth, back and forth. And each time she passed the large mirror on the dressing table, she turned her little head with its shiny ash blonde hair knotted at the nape of her neck, so she could get a glimpse of her broad, beautiful shoulders, and check if her stomach protruded just the right amount. And how snowy white her skin was, creases curving around the front of her throat and a fine golden blush on her cheeks – like a peach, Theodor said. She stopped, out of breath, in front of the living-room mirror and regarded herself with satisfaction.

The dimple in her chin was quite pretty. And so was her little mouth with cherry lips and soft little indentations at the corners, Theodor said. And her nose – pert and straight. And her large, shining, laughing eyes that she narrowed in such an amusing way,

Theodor said – ha,ha,ha, yes, that's what he said. But her teeth and ears were the most charming of all; so Theodor had given her elegant little stones in gold settings with screw backs that fastened to her earlobes.

Yes, things were going very well for her. Soon she would have to see about buying herself some new curtains, because the ones over there were getting too dirty. Heavy linen with wide embroidered tulle borders, not useless little rags like that flimsy gauze. Then she could let Synnøve take the dirty ones home and wash them. Theodor was right, it was more practical to have a housekeeper in the morning to get the dinner and do whatever was needed. A full-time maid would be too much of a bother.

She walked over to the open window, leaned her crossed arms on the sill, and poked her head out, looking toward Ullevålsveien. 'Now I won't move a muscle until I see him.'

'Øvre Bjerregaardsgate,' she read on the sign across the way from her. 'Ugh, all those buildings are the same. I wonder if the street will go right past Gamle Akers Church, when they finally get it finished. Those wheels look like they're sinking all the way into the mud.' She turned her head to follow a cart which was rattling down the bumpy unpaved road, where the mud after the downpour of the last few days was nearly a foot deep.

Outside the house across the street, where some boards had been laid as a walkway, two housemaids were whispering and laughing up at Lucie's window. 'Well go ahead and stare, what do I care.' Lucie tossed her head. 'Really now! Shameless hussies, pointing at people.'

Slamming the window shut, she walked to the kitchen, which was barely equipped with the basic kitchen implements, fixed some bread and butter, and stood and ate it with a glass of water.

'Oh why doesn't he come?' She had gone back to the sitting room and was sitting in the rocking chair, rocking slowly back and forth. 'Sitting around here waiting for him!' It was really mean of him to always keep her waiting.

And suppose he got tired of her and deserted her some day – it would probably turn out just like her mother had predicted, and she'd be the most wretched creature in the world. Her mother, father, sisters

9

and brothers – yes. How were they all? She wouldn't see them any more, because she didn't dare go to Kragerø and none of them would ever come to Kristiania. Oh no, they were plenty busy slaving away and struggling to make a living, especially now that her father had crushed his foot at the shipyard. Now he was getting a smaller daily wage, Jossa had said the day she ran into her. – What did Jossa want in town anyway? They all came here and started gadding around. – Poor old fellow, she felt bad about him, but she didn't care about her mother, because she'd always been so mean and horrid to her. Like the time she came back from the trip to America with Mrs. Thorsen and her children. – Of course it was disgraceful, what had happened to her, but if Mother had had her way, she would have had to give birth in the street. Oh God – the things she had to put up with from Mother during that time! She shivered just thinking about it. – And was it her fault, really? Could she help it that she was so beautiful that men wouldn't leave her alone? She had been properly engaged and everything. Who would have guessed that the ship's mate was such a scoundrel. Oh God, Oh God! The way the fellow had talked her around – begged and carried on, coaxed and had his way with her. Lord help us! And she had held out and said no, even though she loved him so much that she trembled whenever she saw him. Thank God the baby was born dead, so she didn't have that burden! – Oh well. That was life. If he hadn't seduced and deceived her, then she wouldn't be sitting here now. Or if she had gone on with her conversion, running to prayer meetings every evening at the Free Church. She was happy then, but it got so boring in the long run. Then she wouldn't have run off to Kristiania either, started down the wrong path again and taken up with Olsen from the Tivoli orchestra. Ugh, it had been so disgusting when she lived with him. No, she was in a very different situation now, because she was fond of Theodor. She loved him. Yes she truly did. As much as she had loved the ship's mate, it was nothing compared to what she felt for Theodor. And it had been good in some ways that she had gone to Tivoli, because otherwise Theodor would never have even known she existed. He was not the kind of man who was out on the streets at night. He was above that sort of thing.

Would he marry her? Oh no, that was not very likely, although he certainly could, there was no reason why not. She was pretty enough, for sure, and nobody looking at her would guess she wasn't well-born. Theodor had often told her so. And she knew Mrs. Thorsen had told another captain's wife who was on board with them in Quebec, that if she married well, she'd know how to conduct herself. And she had read and learned so much since then. She was at least twice as good now. Of course he could marry her. He was so terribly in love with her, that was what he said, and it was plain as day.

Oh she would be so loving to him, would love him every day of the year, every hour of the day, and submit herself to him. Yes *she* would submit, no matter how he behaved, no matter how he treated her, for she really couldn't expect too much. And faithful! Oh so true to him – as good as gold. What bliss that would be. Yes *that* would be bliss, more than a person could truly bear, and so probably it was best if it didn't happen.

Pooh, happen! Things like that only happened in fairy tales and comedies and the like. Well, a fine, rich man could marry a simple girl perhaps, but not someone who'd been like she was before. If Theodor were still young, but a man like him – 36 years old, a widower and all that. No, she'd just have to stay here. And so Theodor would go off on a trip every holiday, like this summer when she had nearly died of boredom and loneliness, and simply because she didn't know what to do with herself, she'd gone out and started to talk with a fellow. Theodor should know that she actually had to fight him off at the door because when it came right down to it, she didn't want him to come upstairs with her.

Suddenly she jumped to her feet, ran on tiptoes into the front hall where she listened for a moment, then hurried back, wrapped her skirt tightly around herself, and crouched down behind the American wicker chair.

Shortly afterwards there was the sound of footsteps in the front hall, someone opened the door of the sitting room and closed it again; the footsteps entered the bedroom, where they stopped for a moment, then continued into the sitting room. A lazy male voice with a Bergen drawl said, 'Come out, Lucie. I know very well that you're in here someplace.'

He struck a match and lit the gilded hanging lamp. Then he looked around the room, bent down and peeked under the tablecloth. 'She would never…' But then he found her.

With a whoop of laughter, Lucie straightened up and threw her arms around his neck. 'You thought for a minute that I wasn't here!' she cried, kissing him. 'Oh Lord, am I really not allowed to laugh!' she added in a different tone, when she saw him knit his eyebrows in apparent displeasure.

'Well, don't bellow like that. You're much too sweet to be whooping like a mule driver. Besides I expected to find you in bed. You know that's what I like when I come so late.'

Lucie moved away a little. 'Lying there staring at the walls,' she said crossly. 'Why didn't you come earlier?'

'I was delayed.' He grabbed for her hand, but Lucie stuck it behind her back.

'Delayed. You're always saying that.'

'Now don't sulk, Lucie, it doesn't become you. You're so bewitchingly sweet when you smile.' He took her by the waist and pulled her to him. She rested her head against his shoulder, so that he felt her soft hair against his throat.

'Nothing matters as long as you're here,' she said in a soft, tender voice. 'Then everything is good, so good.'

He turned his rather pointed head and looked at her. His smooth brown hair was clipped short at the back and a lock in front fell across a high narrow forehead that was balding at the temples. The deep-set eyes that gazed down at her face were always half closed except when something momentarily excited him. Then he opened them wide.

'My sweet, darling, vagabond troll!' Lucie cried, raising her head, clasping him around the waist with both hands, and pushing her stomach forward to help hoist him off the floor. 'I have to pick you up and carry you, and really play with you, because I love you so much, so much, so much.'

Gasping for air, he got his feet back on the floor and a warm smile spread across his tanned oval face, framed by a dark beard clipped short at the cheeks. On his chin the beard was longer but so sparse that the skin below his bottom lip showed through.

'And you're heavy, too!' Lucie cried, out of breath and red-cheeked. 'But I did get you to laugh a little. Think how odd it is that you almost never laugh, Theodor.'

'You're one of a kind.' Theodor chuckled, smoothing his crumpled pants down over his long, thin legs. 'I may be skinny and small-boned,' he said, straightening his waistcoat and adjusting his watch chain, which was also in disarray, 'but really.'

'You, skinny! You're big and strong, old boy.'

'Oh, I suppose,' he answered, examining his rather sloping shoulders in the mirror. 'I could be worse.'

'But you look like Mephistopheles in the play.' Lucie's face came into view beside his in the mirror. She stood behind him and stretched up on tiptoes so that her chin reached his shoulder. 'The same height and the same chiselled face.'

'You're teasing! It's only the eyebrows.'

'And this?' Lucie drew her forefinger down along his crooked nose, with its firm little nostrils and soft tip. 'But that's the reason I'm so terribly fond of you.' She nuzzled her face up under his beard. 'And also the way you smell.'

'Now, now, you're tickling me. Aren't you going to offer me a glass of wine this evening?'

Lucy ran over to the cupboard.

'But what's this mess doing here, Lucie?' Theodor pointed with an expression of disgust to the tablecloth where there were some strands of hair and a kinky wisp that had obviously been in a braid.

'For heaven's sake,' Lucie said, setting a tray with glasses and bottle on the table. 'It's Nilsen's.'

'She was here again today?' His normally low and rather sleepy voice had taken on an aggrieved tone. 'I can't understand what you want with that disgusting female.'

'She doesn't bother me – the poor scatterbrained old creature.' Lucie grabbed the wisps of hair and stuck them in the stove. 'Remember how kind she's been to me – letting me stay with her two weeks for nothing.'

'Why must I constantly be reminded of that cesspool you were living in – ugh.' Twisting his neck as if his collar were annoying him,

Theodor hooked his thumbs in his waistcoat pockets and started pacing the floor.

Lucie poured wine in the glasses. 'Have a drink now,' she said cheerfully.

'Upon my word, the situation is bad enough as it is,' he went on, getting more and more worked up, 'without the constant aggravation of having you seeking out your old acquaintances. When you know how much I'm against it.' He stopped and gave her a pained, reluctant look.

'Oh yes, you can talk!' Lucie burst out angrily. 'You have your friends and business affairs and women friends and parties and trips, the whole city and everything else, but I – I sit here all day long like some kind of prisoner, without even a cat to keep me company. Thank heavens somebody wants to visit a kept woman like me.'

'Oh really.' He stamped his foot and started pacing again.

'Like this summer when I was here completely alone. I was glad Nilsen came to visit once in a while. If she hadn't come I'd have simply died.'

Mouth clamped shut, his thin red lips nearly invisible, he raised his brows so that the space between the sleepy white eyelids and black arched eyebrows was wider than usual.

'I'm only human, after all,' Lucy continued in an exasperated tone, 'although that obviously doesn't occur to you. And God knows, there are plenty of times when I get so sick of my own company that I just wish I wasn't here.'

He didn't answer, just paced the floor.

'And maybe that would be the best thing, for me to just leave – go down to Copenhagen, or over to America. It's so easy for a person to find something there, and maybe there I could even be respectable.' Lucie stood with her back straight, gripping the table as she spoke.

Without saying a word or glancing at her, Theodor walked with measured steps into the front hall, took his hat and left the house.

'Just as you please, old boy,' Lucie nodded. 'You'll come back. We've seen this before, that's for sure.' She lit a cigarette and lay down on the sofa.

Theodor was firmly resolved to go straight home, but when he got to the end of the street, he turned right instead and went up Ullevålsveien.

A painted woman slipped out of a doorway into the street, her big bold eyes, unkempt bangs and rouged cheeks a glaring contrast to the pale illumination of the summer night. As she was passing Theodor, she stopped and spoke to him.

'Go to Hell,' he said through clenched teeth, stamping the ground so viciously that the woman jumped and retreated with a burst of laughter and a string of obscenities.

He struck out with long strides and a brooding face, and soon passed St. Hanshaugen.

No, there was nothing else he could do; he would just have to marry her. The fact was, he couldn't live without her. That was why he had taken a trip this summer, to wean himself away from her. Did it do any good? Certainly. He was a thousand times more in love when he got back. Risk losing her? The very thought drove him mad. But if he didn't marry her, some day she would surely make good on her threat and leave him, this woman with her proud beauty and sparkling intelligence. Or someone else could get hold of her and lure her away from him. She went out in the street and to the theatre sometimes. He really couldn't absolutely forbid it, but how he suffered when he knew she was out there. This insecurity was utterly destroying him. Getting thin, they said. Indeed, how could it be otherwise in his situation. So why shouldn't he just marry her? Then he'd be done with this tiresome running around at night; after a while it really wore him down. He was, in fact, an independent man in every way, had money enough and a good position; his parents in Bergen had died and his brothers and sisters lived elsewhere. Yes, of course, he should marry her. He would have done it a long time ago if there hadn't been that business of her past. That was and remained a terrible stain on a woman's reputation, and though there was nothing to be done about it, it was so painful, so painful. Yes it was painful, but dear God, at least he knew about it. She had told him everything, down to the last detail. He would have to try to put it behind him. It couldn't be otherwise, and he loved her in spite of it, just exactly as she was.

With his first wife there had been no stain, and he had never noticed he was happier for that. He had been fond of her, very fond of her, and had grieved when she died in childbirth following the stillborn child they had wanted for five years; and when he had buried them both on the same day, he had thought he would never again know happiness in this world. But the joy he felt in Lucie's caresses was something altogether different. Just being near her, seeing her hand or her foot, or when she was lying in bed, her beautiful naked arms reaching out to him – was enough to drive him wild.

Why was he so easily irritated by her? Like tonight. Good God, she was perfectly right, the life she led was like being in prison, a sad life. – Oh yes he understood all right – it was because something was always coming up between them that reminded him of the thing he couldn't bear to think about. – Oh this past of hers, this accursed, accursed past.

He had got all the way up to Vestre Aker before he turned and went back again. He would go to Lucie and make up with her, oh he was burning to see her now. He took long strides, which carried him almost in a run down the hill. It was a good thing nobody saw him.

It was always this way when he was away from her. Every drop of his blood screamed for her, especially when there had been a disagreement between them. Indeed he might as well have spared himself the trouble of going away this evening. He must have known that he'd soon be running like a lunatic to shorten the minutes of separation. His head burning, he took off his hat a couple of times to cool himself and sighed like a person with an uneasy heart. For even now, aglow with love and desire, he recognised simultaneously the muffled ill-will that always rankled within him, the stinging bitterness about his love, the painful jealous hatred toward the ones who had possessed her before him, and ultimately, the annoyance that he, Theodor Gerner, was a captive in a relationship that caused him pain and that he knew he couldn't bear to end. He had gone up there this evening resolved to tell her that she should become his wife, but no sooner had he seen her than he became uncertain and thought it could wait until another time. It was only when he was away from her that it seemed inevitable that they marry. When he was with her he thought things were fine as they were.

Yes that was exactly it. He stood still, his forefinger on his nose. *With* her you are happy, *away* from her you have no peace. What was there for him to think about?

A couple of minutes later he was at her street door, taking out the key he always carried in his pocket. Oh this disgusting entryway, with the inner door to the filthy courtyard always open onto the long numbered row of privy doors directly ahead. And these revolting stairs that reeked of the gutter and kerosene, the narrow pointed windows that were sealed shut, the grey walls that had holes in the plaster and dusty spider webs hanging down like funeral crepe. He was so tired of all of it. These doors on every landing, one on each side and one in the centre, with their crackled porcelain nameplates, smudged calling cards and figured panes of dull glass, the green bell pulls with tattered lace handles, and the ragged mats in front of the doors.

Quickly and silently he let himself into the front hall, hung up his hat and opened the door to the sitting room. God knows why she had lit the lamps, as light as it was, he thought, looking around for Lucie. Oh it would be good not to come to these ugly oblong rooms any more, the pale pink walls and overdone ceilings, and these appalling heating stoves with shelves.

Lucie was lying on the sofa, her arms folded on her breast, staring straight ahead with her eyes wide open. She gave not the slightest sign that she heard him come in.

'Oh, Lucie,' he said tenderly, dragging a chair over to the sofa with his foot and sitting down. 'I can understand of course that it must get lonely for you from time to time, but if you have nothing else, you can always look forward to me.' He leaned over her and kissed her.

She threw an arm around his neck and pressed her lips to his mouth so hard she felt his kiss on her teeth.

'Oh God, I love you so, Theodor,' she whispered. 'Oh you have no idea, even though you're so mean and horrid toward me.' She tweaked his earlobes. 'Why are you like that, you horrible thing.'

'You don't pay enough attention to how you behave, my sweet.

17

You know very well that you're the one who always provokes me. But just the same, you're the dearest person in the world to me. Come now, I want to go to bed and then I'll tell you something in confidence.' He straightened up with a hasty movement and pushed the table aside to give her room. At that instant his eye fell on Nilsen's letter, which Lucie had laid on top of her sewing basket.

'What is this?' He picked up the letter and read, 'Dear, precious girl!'

'A love letter, as you can see perfectly well.' Lucie had begun to unbutton her dress and went into the bedroom, leaving the door open behind her. Are we starting in on Nilsa again? she thought.

After Theodor had read the letter, he let it drop onto the table, took out his elegant red-bordered handkerchief and wiped his fingers carefully with it. He stood for a moment, sunk in thought, with a dark, anxious expression in his hooded eyes.

'Aren't you coming now, Theodor!' He heard the rustle of the feather mattress as Lucie hopped into bed. 'There's no need to make such a fuss about that stupid letter.'

Gerner passed his hand over his face and went into the bedroom.

'Why haven't you told me you have a suitor?' he asked, sitting down on chair by the bed.

'Oh you really are too funny, Theodor! You don't really think that!' She burst into laughter.

'It's most deplorable that you don't have more confidence in me,' Gerner continued. 'I really have deserved more than that from you. Letting them propose to you like that. Who is this pup?'

Lucie had stopped laughing. Her heart was beating violently and her voice sounded a little tight when she answered: 'He does errands for the people at Tivoli in the afternoon and in the morning he's a messenger for a bank or something.'

'Have – you had – a relationship – with him in the past?' It sounded as if it pained him to get the words out.

'He's never laid a finger on me, not ever. You always think that.'

'When did these proposals of his start?'

'It was a while ago,' Lucy said in an embarrassed tone.

'And you let him continue! You only needed to say a word to me.

18

I would have told him to keep his nose away from you. Why were you so quiet about it?'

'I didn't want anything to do with him then. You can see that from the letter.'

'*Then.* What do you mean by that?'

'A person does have to think about the future,' she said querulously. 'What's going to become of me?'

'Could you really bring yourself to marry that person?'

'That would be the most sensible thing, I suppose.'

Gerner sat quite still, with his face turned toward Lucie, gazing over at her in the dusk of the summer night. She was lying on her back, with her throat and arms bare, fiddling with the covers.

'It doesn't happen very often that an honest man wants to marry someone like me.' Lucie spoke with pauses between the words. 'And is it really so strange if I think, you'll just have to accept it, there's not going to be anything else for you in life, and in time you'll forget Theodor, if you try very hard.'

'Have you answered the letter, Lucie?' There was something in his tone that made her tremble in anticipation, but she answered him quite calmly, 'No, not yet.'

'Then write and tell him that in a fortnight you're going to marry someone else.'

Joy flooded through her entire body in a warm stream; she almost uttered a cry of jubilation, but with a hurried effort she managed to say indifferently, 'Why should I tell him a lie?'

'I came up here this evening to tell you that I intend to marry you as soon as possible.'

'Is that true, Theodor, is it really true?' She sat up, grasped his head and looked at him with large frightened eyes. 'You mustn't play games with me, Theodor, I can't bear it.'

'I'm not. The matter is much too serious for that. I've thought about it so much. There's no resisting it. I hope you never give me grounds to regret it.'

She threw herself against him with a muffled cry, pressed her head to his chest, and bursting into violent sobs, said, 'I'll die of joy, Theodor!'

When Gerner quietly left the apartment at dawn, Lucie sat bolt upright in bed, and with beaming eyes and warm flushed cheeks, listened until his footsteps faded down the stairs. The morning light flooded into the room from the casement windows, outlining each object with strangely sharp contours.

Lucie clasped her hands, stretched her arms above her head, and exhaled a long, drawn-out 'aahh.' 'Mrs. Gerner, Mrs. Lucie Gerner,' she said, bouncing up and down on the rustling feather mattress and clapping her hands together. 'Mrs. Theodor Gerner, Mrs. Gerner the lawyer's wife! Oh my, oh my, oh my.'

Finally she lay back in bed with her face turned toward the room and her hands clasped under her chin. 'To think that Nilsa's letter would have such happy results. I'll never forget that. Mrs. Gerner. Mrs. Lucie Gerner.'

Lying there, giggling at the large, blue-rimmed water jar that Gerner had put down on the floor by the washstand, she was wide-awake and animated, as after a long restorative sleep.

II
After the Honeymoon

'Lord, how awkward this is! Now we won't be able to see him socially any more.' Mrs. Mørk was speaking. She stood in the elegant waiting room of her husband, Doctor Aksel Mørk, wearing her hat and cape, holding an embroidered basket in her hand.

'Oh, why not?' Mørk straightened up at his desk and leaned his large round balding head on the backrest of the upholstered armchair.

'We can't invite him to anything but gentlemen's parties, because surely you aren't going to force me to associate with that kind of woman?' Mrs. Mørk's pale moist eyes had a fierce expression.

'Now that she's married, she is not that kind of woman, but my friend Theodor Gerner's wife, and as such, she is naturally welcome in our house.'

'Well, for a man I don't suppose it matters so much,' Mrs. Mørk said, lifting her long pointed nose in the air. 'You're accustomed to all kinds of things, of course.'

Mørk grunted and clamped his thin lips together as he stroked his clean-shaven cheeks.

'But good heavens,' said his wife, tucking her smooth, blond hair under the brim of her hat, 'if that's what you want, then I know that's the way it will be. A wife has no say in the matter.'

'You'd better go now, otherwise you'll be late for the boat.' Mørk picked up the pen he'd put down.

'Aren't you coming out tonight to look at Ba? He had a terrible cough last night.'

'If I have time, but right now while the meeting is going on, you know how busy I am. I'll come out to see you tomorrow.'

'Oh yes, I'm sure you will,' Mrs. Mørk snapped. She walked over and put her hand on the door handle. 'You'll be having much too much fun for that, I imagine. We'll see if you ever get me to spend the summer in the country again.' She stood there for a minute, moving her foot back and forth across the floor with a sweeping sound. Her lips were pursed and her light eyebrows, which looked like they'd recently been plucked, were drawn together in a frown.

'Aren't you going to say goodbye to me, Aksel?' she asked in a sulky voice.

'The one who leaves is supposed to say goodbye, isn't that right?' Mørk replied good-naturedly.

She ran up behind him on tiptoe, threw her arms around his neck and kissed him. 'Goodbye then, you monster – don't be angry with me because I was cross just now, but you always irritate me so.'

A tired expression crossed Mørk's face and a little sigh escaped him, but a moment later he smiled and patted her cheek. 'Yes Sophie, you do have a hard time,' he joked.

'Oh you!' she tossed her head. 'But now you'll see, I'll be very sweet and nice to her, this woman of Gerner's. But then you'll have to appreciate it, Aksel, because God knows, I'm doing it for your sake. Goodbye, now.'

An hour later when Mørk was walking down Universitetsgaten, he recognised Gerner a few steps ahead.

'Pst, pst, Gerner, hello!'

Gerner stopped and turned around.

'You're already back from your honeymoon! You took care of that in a hurry. I guess I'd better congratulate you then!' Mørk shook Gerner's hand.

Gerner nodded and looked embarrassed.

'So that's why we've seen so little of you lately,' Mørk continued as they walked down the street together. 'Well, I'd heard you had a pretty little bird in a cage somewhere, but I would have sworn you weren't thinking about getting married.'

'What the hell,' Gerner shrugged his shoulders. 'A man's not his own master in such matters, for God's sake. You don't do it because you *want* to, but because you can't help it.'

'Oh well, it's not absolutely certain that you're going to regret it either.' Mørk's tone was a little despondent.

'Regret it,' said Gerner, flinching as if he'd been stuck by a needle. 'The day comes when you regret everything, especially the things you didn't do. What's the use of arranging your life so you do nothing you won't regret? Tell that to people when they start having children, for instance. What could be more reckless than reproducing yourself – yourself! – when you know yourself all too well. And to do it in a time like this, in a world like ours.'

'You old pessimist!' Mørk slapped Gerner on the back. 'And here I thought you'd had a conversion.'

'Well, you're supposed to lose your head when you're contemplating matrimony, but it hasn't been quite that bad with me.' Gerner smiled so broadly that his nose dipped down over his moustache.

'Ah yes, Theodor old boy, God help you! Marriage is and will always be a big lottery for us men. We'd be better off if we could steer clear of it, but we simply can't.' Mørk sighed.

'No, but in this case there really is a chance that it will go well,' Gerner said. 'She feels boundless gratitude toward me and is utterly dependent. I have, so to speak, created and invented her. She is young and soft as wax, I can make her into whatever I want.' They had stopped at the end of the street.

'Well, goodbye then,' Mørk said. 'You'll have to bring your wife over, of course, or perhaps we're the ones who should... Well, Sophie will take care of it.'

'Do you know if Mrs. Reinertson is in town these days?' Gerner asked, releasing Mørk's hand.

'No, though my wife did say she came up to our apartment looking for a book today. But if you want to see her, it's probably best to go out to Malmø. Goodbye, and remember that at *our home* your wife is welcome.'

'Goodbye.'

'*Our home*,' Gerner repeated to himself as he walked down Karl Johan. The emphasis Mørk placed on those words had offended him. He assumed it was necessary to reassure him that they wouldn't shut their doors on her. Well, he'd have to be prepared for his old friends to turn up their noses at Lucie. But there was Mrs. Reinertson at least. She would welcome her with open arms and perhaps the others would follow suit. A lady like Mrs. Reinertson was good to have as an ally.

When Gerner arrived at his house on Incognitogaten, he met Mrs. Reinertson on the steps leading down from his apartment. She'd been up to say hello to the newlyweds, she said. Gerner extended his hand with a grateful smile and tried to read in her face the kind of impression Lucie had made on her. But Mrs. Reinertson was in a hurry, on her way out of town on the one o'clock boat.

'Lord, Mrs. Reinertson is so charming and sweet,' Lucie said after Gerner had settled himself in the sitting room. 'She really is very unusual, don't you agree, Theodor?'

Gerner had begun to detest Lucie's eternal 'don't you agree, Theodor,' a habit she'd adopted after the wedding. And she said 'Theodor' with three different inflections.

'Funny that she didn't get married again, don't you agree, Theodor?'

'She probably didn't want to,' Theodor said taking a newspaper from the table.

'Why didn't you fall in love with her, Theodor? Your first wife's cousin – it would have been so convenient.'

Gerner shrugged his shoulders.

'Imagine, she kissed me at the door and said she hoped we'd become good friends.'

'Well, she's a bit emotional,' Gerner replied, his eyes on the newspaper.

'Wasn't that terribly sweet though, Theodor? Imagine, I thought it was touching, don't you agree, Theodor?'

Gerner muttered something unintelligible.

'When was it that you spent so much time at the Mørks' house, Theodor?' Lucie was sitting across from her husband with her arms on the table. She was in high spirits. 'I thought you said you didn't see them very often because Sara didn't like them. Didn't you say that, Theodor?'

'After her death we got together again the same as before,' he forced himself to say. The familiarity of Lucie's reference to Sara, his first wife, annoyed him.

'Just think how late Mørk got married,' Lucie rambled on. 'Or maybe he was a widower like you, Theodor?'

'No, he'd never been married before.'

'Is it a happy marriage, do you suppose?'

Theodor was engrossed in the newspaper.

'She's not a bit pretty, not in the photograph at least, but young I suppose, and gentlemen are always after young blood, especially when they're getting old, like you, Theodor.' She laughed merrily and went on, 'Mrs. Mørk did have lots of money, but she's not from a really fine family, isn't that right, Theodor?'

Gerner couldn't stand it any longer. Ugh, that vulgar laugh of hers. 'I'm going to take a walk before dinner,' he said, standing up abruptly.

'I'll go with you!' she cried happily. 'This is when all the fine people are out walking on Drammensveien.'

'I don't want to be with all those people.'

'No, it's much more fun to walk up Bogstadveien; we'll have it more to ourselves. Isn't it wonderful that we're man and wife now, Theodor?' She ran after him, hung on his arm and lifted her lips for a kiss. Pretending not to see, he walked out to the front hall and put on his coat.

'Are you coming?' he asked after a few moments. He poked his head through the open door but didn't see her.

'No, I don't want to after all; you go, Theodor.' Her tone of voice had changed completely.

She didn't know what had made her so depressed, but she felt such a torment of restlessness that she couldn't stay still and had to keep shifting from place to place. She had been so happy and contented and now that was all swept away. Just because Theodor hadn't covered her with kisses and caresses the way he usually did. Of course a person couldn't always behave the same way. Maybe she'd been chattering too much. Theodor wasn't very talkative, of course, but in the old days he'd said he was so fond of her chirping.

When he got back, she would be quieter and more serious and see if he didn't like that better.

But an hour and a half later when Theodor returned home, he was as loving and affectionate as ever. He came right over and embraced her and kissed her until she cried that she couldn't breathe. And after dinner she lay in his arms on the chaise longue while he drank coffee and smoked his cigar.

There was a flurry of parties and visits now. Lucie was radiantly happy from morning to evening and scarcely had time to think about the spells of coolness and remoteness that came over Theodor from time to time.

As winter approached and things quieted down a bit, Theodor suggested that she take English lessons from a lady who advertised her services; it would give her something serious to do. Lucie happily agreed and enthusiastically set to work.

During the course of the winter she became somewhat thinner and paler, but the change was very becoming. People had to admit that whatever else could be said about her – the little 'Tivoli-wife' was certainly beautiful.

III
At Home

Lucie collected the punch glasses on a tray and carried it from the card-table in Theodor's room to the dining room. Then she stacked the counters in the boston box, moved the candles over to the desk and put the cards away. Her hands were trembling slightly and her face looked pale and strained. From the front hall she heard voices saying farewell. The card party was leaving. When Gerner came back from seeing his guests to the door, Lucie was wiping off the card-table. She gave him a searching look. Gerner's face was dark and there was a scornful lift to his eyebrows. He took a box of matches and went into the bedroom.

Lucie stood stiff and silent, her fingers clenched around the dust cloth. Then she walked over and put it in the basket along the wall by the tile stove, picked it up again immediately and started to wipe the table again, dropped it on the floor, and then walked slowly, stopping between every second and third step, into the bedroom.

'Are you angry with me, Theodor?' she asked, pausing just inside the door and fingering her brooch.

He was standing in his shirtsleeves by the washstand with his back turned to Lucie, washing his beard.

'Oh, tell me what's wrong,' she begged timidly.

'You must tell me what's wrong, don't you see?' she continued after waiting for him to dry his face. 'How else will I know how to behave another time?'

'It is completely hopeless,' he answered coldly. 'You'll never be any different.' He poured water into a glass and brushed his teeth.

'Oh no, don't say that, Theodor – I can't bear to hear you say

27

that.' Her voice sounded tearful. 'What's going to become of me if you won't even scold me?'

'I've called your attention to similar things a hundred times before.' He had thrown on his dressing gown and was pacing the floor. 'But it's in your blood.'

'Oh no, Theodor, no, Theodor.' She was biting the corner of her handkerchief while the tears ran down her cheeks.

'Instead of being quiet and modest, your behaviour is downright loud and unrestrained,' Gerner continued. 'When Mørk raised his glass to you, you immediately clinked glasses with him, like you were with a bunch of men who were buying you drinks in a tavern – and with a clink that could have broken the glass. – It's extremely embarrassing.'

'I never thought there could be anything wrong in clinking glasses with someone. Even Mrs. Reinertson does that.'

'And you're comparing yourself with Mrs. Reinertson? A woman who's belonged to good society from the time she was in her cradle. What is respectable high-spirits for her, becomes vulgar in you. Let's not have you mimicking a lady like Mrs. Reinertson.'

'I didn't think about that, Theodor,' Lucie said meekly.

'No, you have no idea what it means to show good manners and discretion. It sounded as if you were complaining that Martine couldn't prepare food that was fine enough for you.'

'No, I didn't do that, Theodor!' Lucie cried.

'When Mørk praised the sauce, you had the nerve to say, with the air of a connoisseur, that you preferred it prepared with wine and truffles. Where have *you* had truffles? Could you possibly be trying to make people believe you were brought up on truffles and the like? Both Mørk and Bugge were quite uncomfortable and they quickly changed the subject to ease the situation for me. And this habit you have of nudging a man and taking his arm when you talk to him.'

Lucie was mortified. The incident with the truffles was extremely embarrassing and she knew very well that she had said it to put on airs. Her face burned as she stood by the door, drawing lines on the carpet with the tip of her shoe.

'But as soon as you start drinking wine you lose all self-restraint.'

Gerner took off his dressing gown, moved the lamp over to the clothes stand, undressed, and got into bed. 'I've said it before and asked you to be careful, but you still guzzle it down, and your spirits get higher with every glass. High spirits do not become you.'

He took from the clothes stand a book that had *Athenæum* stamped in gilded letters on its black cloth binding, opened it to the middle where a letter marked his place, and started to read.

Lucie stood there without moving. Then she went over and kneeled down by Theodor's bed, gently stroked his hand and whispered, 'I'm sorry that I'm such a cause of grief to you, Theodor.'

He kept his eyes on the book and didn't move a muscle. Lucie went on caressing his hand, repeating the same words as she imploringly looked up at his face. Then she bent her head over his hand and moved her lips across it until at last there wasn't a spot on his hand that she hadn't kissed.

'Will you once and for all learn to be more careful then?' he said at last, putting the book down and stroking her hair. 'You do understand that I'm trying to educate you for your own good.'

'Yes, Theodor, sweet, kind Theodor, I understand that so well, so well.' She crept on her knees to the head of the bed, slipped one arm under his head and the other around his shoulders, and hid her face in his neck. 'I understand so well, so well, Theodor, but you must be good and kind to me, Theodor.' Her voice was muffled because she was fighting tears. 'I'd do anything, anything for you, Theodor, gladly die for you, Theodor, because you know…' The words were choked by her sobs.

'There, there, my darling Lucie. Dry your tears and kiss me. I'm not at all angry with you – I just feel so badly for you, my darling Lucie. But it will get better, you'll learn as time goes by, you'll see.'

IV
On the Street

One morning a week later Lucie accompanied Theodor to his office. It was slippery and treacherous underfoot and Lucie laughed merrily every time she escaped a fall by clinging to Theodor's arm. Putting his feet down carefully, he advanced unsteadily on long thin legs in elegant grey-striped trousers, and as he took each step he jabbed his walking stick through the new layer of snow into the transparent sheet of ice below.

'We're sure to break an arm or leg, you know, ooops!' He slipped and almost fell down. 'It's a good thing I brought money so I can pay the cab driver when he takes us to the hospital.'

'This won't do, Theodor, you're too funny. I'm laughing so hard I'm going to fall down right now.'

At the end of Drammensveien they met a gentleman who said hello to Gerner. Lucie returned his greeting, and because she was laughing just then at something Theodor had said, her manner was particularly friendly and smiling.

'Why do you smile and laugh in that forward way with men you don't know?' Gerner said with displeasure. The painful thought had occurred to him that Lucie might have known him from before.

'I just said hello,' Lucie replied boldly.

'You have absolutely no need to say hello to men you haven't been introduced to.'

'Oh what difference does it make, Theodor? When I'm holding your arm it just seems natural, don't you agree, Theodor?'

'And the way you did it! What the man must have thought. – In the future, don't say hello to people you don't know.'

'There are times when you have to, though. – When I meet a lady I know and she's walking with a man, he greets me even if I've never seen him before.'

'That is a completely different situation. You don't understand anything.'

'No, of course not, that's one thing I do know,' Lucie said, offended.

'You've got to break these bad habits,' Gerner continued. 'They're not appropriate in your present position.'

'How nice something happened so you could give me a lecture – otherwise you'd probably think something was missing. Don't you agree, Theodor?'

Lucie was a little frightened by her impertinence, but she was seething inside and couldn't stop herself.

Gerner detached his arm from Lucie's. He needed his hand to take out his handkerchief.

'If the occasion had passed without any manifestation of your old habits, I would have been surprised, at any rate,' he replied icily.

'You're so crude, always harping on the same thing. Is *that* how a gentleman acts?'

Gerner was so astonished that he scarcely believed his own ears. How dare she say that to you, he thought indignantly, blowing his nose and putting his handkerchief away.

They were just past the university now. The temperature was milder here so the snow and ice had thawed a bit and it wasn't as slippery underfoot. Gerner strode off with long measured steps, supported by his cane. Lucie glanced at him timidly. She didn't dare take his arm. A couple of times she quickened her pace so she could talk to him, but when she saw his dark expression and scornful eyelids, she felt as if her tongue were paralysed.

He didn't answer.

She repeated the question.

'I don't know,' he said curtly.

'I beg your pardon, Theodor. Don't be angry with me, Theodor.' She said the words to herself again and again, but no words passed her lips.

'Oh God, we're already at Slottsgaten. In five minutes he'll walk through the entryway and you won't have apologised. Maybe he won't even say goodbye? Oh God, two minutes – one minute, half a minute – a few seconds. – There he goes.'

Lucie stood in the open entryway and watched Theodor walk across the flagstones. He turned left at a set of stone steps and disappeared.

'Goodbye, Theodor!' she cried after him. It sounded like a scream. Then her feelings surged up and overflowed. She quickly slipped into the angle behind the wooden door, drew a handkerchief out of her muff, covered her face and sobbed.

'Really nothing to get so furious about, after all,' she comforted herself when she was out on the street a short while later. 'Carrying on like that because you say one little word. – You've got the right to say one little word, after all.'

'It's Luciekins! Oh, what fun that I finally run into her.' Lucie felt somebody grab her by the shoulders, then something soft, a tickle of hair on her cheek, and directly in her path, she saw Nilsen's grey face under a dotted veil, the feathers of her hat bobbing down over her hair.

'Take your muff away,' Lucie said, averting her face.

'Well, how are you doing, Luciekins? Everything's wonderful, I suppose?'

'Yes, thank you,' Lucie said absentmindedly, wondering how she could get rid of her.

'Which way are you going, Luciekins?'

'Up the street.'

'Then I'll walk with you a bit. I want to promenade with you, Luciekins. My stock goes up when I walk beside such a queenly coat, yes by God!' She laughed and bit her thick lower lip. 'Silk plush with sealskin trim and matching hat! Oh God, other people's clothes look like rags.' She glanced sadly down at her own worn garment, a tight-fitting coat with ancient mock fur trim, and gave her cat skin muff a shake. 'But as long as you've got a fashionable hat and a pair of decent gloves, I always say. – Isn't it strange to be so happy, Luciekins?'

'But what did *I* tell you?' she continued without waiting for an answer. 'Do you remember, we made a bet the last time I was at your house, that time last summer when I got so offended.' She pursed her lips, sniffled a bit, and assumed a shamefaced expression.

'Yes, I do owe you a gift for that bet,' Lucie said.

'So she does, so she does, but there's no hurry – it's nice to have something coming.'

'How is Errand-Christiansen these days?' Lucie asked.

'He got married, the lazy oaf,' Nilsen said contemptuously. 'He finally got a blind old washerwoman to take pity on him.'

'So you're spared the unwelcome company.'

'Spared unwelcome company! Oh no, my dear.' Nilsen shook her head mournfully.

'He's still after you, even afterwards?'

'Not him, but others, ha, ha, ha! Men are completely obsessed you know, yes, by God. And they're so disgusting, Lucie, they always want something bad, they do.' She took a couple of skipping steps and repeated, 'Yes, they do.'

'Walk normally,' Lucie said. 'People are turning around.'

'They do that anyway. I can't walk down the street anymore without them staring – no, by God. It must be my tragic profile, ha, ha, ha! Olsen says... but I won't tell you about him, since you haven't asked about him,' she added with a nod and a guarded expression.

'Ugh, that old goat – spare me. Well I have to say goodbye, now.' Lucie stopped at the corner of Universitetsgaten. 'I'm visiting someone close by.'

'I'll walk you to the door, Luciekins. Does she think I'll let go of her so easily once I've finally got my claws in her?'

There was nothing else to do. Lucie had to continue walking with her. But in which one of these buildings should she pretend to have an errand?

'Believe me, I've often wanted to come visit you, Lucie, so I could have a look at your palace. But I didn't dare, no, by God. – I was so afraid of your husband.'

'He won't bite your head off, you know,' Lucie said.

'He looks so stern, like a Roman monk-prince,' she pronounced the words with a deep, solemn voice. 'I'll never forget the way he bowed to me, that time he came when I was visiting you. – Such manners! And the way he looked at me sideways with those aristocratic eyes of his – hee!' She squealed as if she were being tickled. 'He could lead you into the abyss – yes by God, into the abyss. Is he terribly in love with you, hmm? Does he squeeze you and crush you and eat you up, hmm? With his tongue hanging out of his mouth, hmm?' She minced along with her muff clasped to her stomach, repeating breathlessly, 'Hmm, hmm, hmm?'

'Here's where I'm going,' Lucie said, stopping by the building where the Mørks and Mrs. Reinertson lived.

'But I'm coming up to see my princess. You'll let me, won't you?' She spoke in a wheedling tone and cocked her head.

'Yes, of course, you really must! How silly that you were afraid to. Would *I* put on airs because I've come up in the world? And my husband! Do you think he wouldn't be friendly and sweet to his wife's old girlfriend? He loves me too much for that.' Lucie spoke excitedly. It was as if her mouth were speaking on its own, saying what she knew Nilsen expected her to say; it was also the prospect of getting rid of her, getting some kind of reprieve, that made her so extremely effusive. 'You really must come, do you hear. I'll be insulted if you don't come,' she added finally.

Nilsen, nodding and smiling, had melted completely. 'Bless my soul, you're so sweet, Lucie! But suppose you weren't home or I met your husband alone – I'd faint, by God, I would. Couldn't you come get me some day? I live at number 20, Øvre Slottsgate.'

'The building next to my husband's office?'

'Yes, the back of the courtyard, all the way up on the third floor. The stairs are dark and horrid, but that won't bother my angel Lucie, I'm sure of that.'

'No, not at all. I'll come some day,' Lucie said quickly.

'There's a sign on the door, so you won't get lost. God bless her, what a sweetie she is! If I have to pawn all of Madame Kling's furniture, I'll have a nice treat to serve you.'

'Well, goodbye then, I have to hurry now,' Lucie shook her hand for the third time.

'I'll walk up and down the street and wait for a while!' Nilsen called after her. 'Because she may not be home, the lady you want to see.'

'That's all I need,' Lucie muttered. She had planned to stand in the stairway for a bit and when she figured Nilsen was gone, slip out and go home by way of Christian Augustsgate and Castle Park – Nilsa was the worst leech in the world.

If only she could think of an errand at Mrs. Reinertson's – she stood there in a quandary half way up the steps. Yes of course, she could say she'd heard that a washerwoman lived in the basement and ask if Mrs. Reinertson knew whether she did good work.

V

At Mrs. Reinertson's

Pastor Brandt from Arendal was in Kristiania paying a short visit to his sister, Mrs. Reinertson. He was just finishing a late breakfast; Mrs. Reinertson had left the table and was tending to the plants.

'I think you'd better give me a little glass of cognac,' the pastor said, and a minute later, 'There's something wrong with us Bergen people, you know. We're too lyrical, too easily caught up in the moment. – If only there were no such thing as the day after.' He held his large, handsome forehead in both hands.

Mrs. Reinertson retrieved a bottle and a glass from the buffet and poured him a glass. Then she returned to the plants.

'You've still got the same swing in your walk, Karen.' Brandt had emptied the glass in one gulp. 'Put your shoulders into it, as our dear departed mother used to say. It's strange how old habits hang on.' He ran his fingers through his thick brown sideburns and straightened his white necktie while examining himself with narrowed eyes in the mirror between the windows.

'Hennessey is the best cognac. It's truly an elixir of life.' He poured himself another half a glass. 'One needs fortification after all these festivities. It comes with age – we aren't as young as we were.'

'No, we'll be old people soon,' Karen said.

'And yet I feel so young at heart, even though I've been a widower for four years come autumn. Is there any more coffee, Karen?'

Karen came over to the table and filled his cup.

'One really shouldn't be a widower – it's not healthy.' Brandt glared down at the coffee cup into which he'd poured cream. 'You live a more regular life when you're married. And then there's the problem that no one really looks after you; you have to fend for yourself – you most certainly do. You scarcely have the benefit of your own child. Mads spends much more time with the grandparents than at home, even though I've got a housekeeper in the house now – they've been nagging me about that for ages.'

'Are you thinking about getting married, Fredrik?' Karen sat down at the table across from him.

Pastor Brandt leaned back in his chair, looked up at the ceiling and uttered a thick braying laugh. 'Yes, why not? Forty isn't really so old for a man, though for my part, I wouldn't think anything of it if you married again at 36. I'm not as narrow-minded as that, thank God.'

'If only you could find someone you wanted,' Karen said laughing.

'And who wanted you; that's just as important, my dear,' Brandt replied with a sigh.

'I'll have a cigarette then,' Karen said when she saw that Brandt had taken a cigar out of his waistcoat pocket and was cutting the tip. 'I waited because I didn't know if you were finished eating.'

'Do you know what I've always wondered about, Fredrik?' Karen continued after she'd lit her cigarette. 'That you can be so lively and cheerful even though you're a pastor and a believer, more or less.'

'More or less!' Brandt laughed heartily with the same thick sound as before. 'That's marvelous. You can be sure, by the way, that I'm watched and pursued down there in that hole of a town. Oh yes!'

'By the unmarried girls, I assume?'

'By them, too,' he snickered – 'and by the pietists! They're after me from all sides because of my worldly life, as they call it – oh, yes! They come in packs to renounce their membership in the State Church, because they want to leave the congregation and have a personal relationship with Christ. Yes indeed, that's what they say. They've got nerve.'

'Don't you caution them about leaving the congregation?'

'Never!' Brandt thrust out his slim white hand. 'I've had enough of that, believe me. Caution that bunch of biddies, with and without skirts, who troop up with their Bibles under their arms and want to teach both the preacher and the deacon. – You'd have to be quite mad.

'So I say, you want a personal relationship with Christ do you? Well now, that's very nice. Go right ahead. The Lord be with you. And then I take out the register and strike their names from the book by the dozens. Don't you understand, Karen, that it's to my credit that I haven't become a prime example of an old countrified pastor under such conditions? If only I had a wife to share my worries with.

'Speaking of wives – what's she like, that girl Theodor Gerner married. Pretty, I suppose?'

'Yes, indeed! Almost a beauty.'

'It's disgusting, in any case.' Brandt retracted his lips above his gums, straining to see his white teeth in the mirror. 'Married to *our* cousin, and then taking up with a person like that afterwards. Shameful!'

'You're not talking like a pastor, Fredrik.'

'Like a pastor. I suppose you think a man is different from other men inside because he's had the misfortune, or fortune, of becoming a pastor? But look here – one's *bride* should be pure in any case, by God!'

'Yes, to be worthy of the bridegroom,' Karen said, taking a long puff on her cigarette.

'What nonsense,' Brandt said and then he began to list examples from the Old Testament of patriarchs and others upon whom the Lord had bestowed innocent virgins so that they might enjoy them and beget offspring.

Karen listened to this with a sarcastic smile, thinking that Our Lord must have been quite a procurer in those days.

The maid came in and announced that Mrs. Gerner was asking for the mistress.

'Show her into the sitting room,' Karen said. 'Isn't this interesting, Fredrik – you'll be able to see her right now.'

> You ask who she favours, and if she is fair,
> The woman I've chosen for my bride.

Singing softly to himself, Brandt paced the floor blowing smoke rings after Karen had gone to greet Lucie.

> Yes, she's as fair as the flowers in spring,
> As holy and pure as God's angels on high
> And as joyous as birdsong in the sky.

He put down his cigar butt and walked into the sitting room.

'Let me introduce you: Mrs. Gerner, my brother, Pastor Brandt from Arendal.'

Lucie raised herself halfway in her chair. Brandt bowed stiffly without extending his hand.

'Nasty outside,' he said, sitting down a little distance away. 'How is your husband?'

'Very well, thank you,' Lucie replied.

'Please give him my regards, and tell him that it's too bad I didn't get to see him. My time is always too short here.'

'Yes, I imagine you've had a lot of things to take care of, Pastor,' Lucie said obligingly. 'It's always that way when you're visiting.'

'*The Gauntlet*,'* said Brandt, putting down the book he had picked up from the table and opened. 'It's a good book.'

'Do you think so?' Karen raised her eyebrows slightly.

'Absolutely. It's the greatest victory for Christianity we've had in a long time. Just think, that an apostle of scepticism is impelled, forced, to preach the eternal truths, Christianity's first and most important commandment, so to speak. Against his will, of course – that's where the strength of the victory lies.'

Karen smiled.

'But don't you see the greatness, the overwhelming greatness in it – the Holy Spirit chastening the sceptics to be workers in the Lord's vineyard? That book is an instrument that will strengthen people's belief and make it as firm as a rock.'

'They're getting it cheaply, I must say', Karen said.

'This conjunction between heathenism and Christianity is an omen that the millennium prophesied in *Revelations* will soon be upon us.' Brandt spoke in an unctuous tone of voice.

'Well, when the seventh commandment is being supported by all this *Gauntlet* talk, I suppose it's possible some good will come of it,' Karen replied, looking at Brandt through narrowed eyes.

'The harvest will be richer! Yes – oh, yes. The believers will be the first to yield to the demand for chastity.'

'If even the freethinkers don't dare tell the truth,' Karen interrupted, 'then society, with all its hypocrisy and hidden vices, will be a thousand times worse.'

'For shame, Karen, how you talk!' Brandt sent a wary, sidelong glance at Lucie.

'And suppose all this nonsense from *The Gauntlet* were obeyed,' Karen continued in a scornful, hurried voice, 'because that is the idea, isn't it, that it *ought* to be, it's not *just* supposed to be hung up as an ideal, is it? If men abstained from that kind of thing until they could get married, when they're thirty or so, and I'm not even taking all the bachelors into account, surely they'd be so weaned from the whole business that they'd never in the world go off and get married. Why should they take on the burden of marriage when they'd already managed for so long?'

'That beats everything,' Brandt said, standing up and pulling out his pocket watch, which was hanging on a long gold lady's watch chain outside his waistcoat. 'I'd better be going. Goodbye, Mrs. Gerner.' He bowed to Lucie. 'I'll see you later, Karen. Don't expect me for dinner.'

I ought to go now, Lucie thought, shortly after Brandt had taken his leave. Mrs. Reinertson had such a preoccupied look – she must be tired of her. She picked up her muff, but then Mrs. Reinertson directed her shining oval eyes right at Lucie and said, 'I would so very much like to be a friend to you, out of sheer egoism, you understand – here I am without children, without a husband. So one busies oneself with other people. Be careful you're not being intrusive, Karen, I always tell myself.'

'You certainly don't need to worry about that, when you're so...' Confused, Lucie stopped and lowered her eyes.

'Do you really like me?' Mrs. Reinertson asked with animation. 'Because I'm so used to people thinking I'm eccentric, or whatever it is they say, that I'm positively delighted when I notice that somebody likes me.'

'She means *me*, me, a woman who's been... she knows about it and just the same...' Lucie was so overcome that tears started welling up. 'You're so alone,' Mrs. Reinertson went on. 'I don't suppose you have any relatives or real women friends, oh, please don't be hurt,' she said imploringly when she saw that Lucie was blushing clear up to her forehead. 'I mean well, and I want you to know once and for all that your so-called past doesn't bother me. Quite the opposite, I'd almost say. So, now it's over, now it's not awkward any more, on the contrary, you're relieved that we've spoken openly about this; you've been worried what people will think about it. Isn't that right?'

'Yes,' Lucie said with quivering lips. The look she gave Mrs. Reinertson went straight to her heart.

'In any event, now you know there's at least one person you needn't be afraid of. One is little enough, but it's something. I've wanted to tell you this for a long time, but there hasn't been an opportunity.'

'How good and kind you are,' Lucie said. 'I didn't know anyone could be like that.'

'I was so happy, yes really, when Theodor Gerner told me he was going to marry you. Naturally, things can go wrong, but the road has at least been cleared of one prime impediment to happiness. Do you understand?'

'Yes,' said Lucie, though it wasn't true, and she was too embarrassed to admit it.

'The road has at least been cleared of one prime impediment to happiness,' Lucie repeated to herself as she walked down the steps. What could Mrs. Reinertson have meant by that? Lucie's eyes were shining and she felt like a person who has been to confession and received a promise of merciful forgiveness for all her sins.

She was so preoccupied with her visit to Mrs. Reinertson's that she didn't think about the quarrel with Theodor until she was back home and heard his steps in the front hall at dinnertime. Then it suddenly came back to her. Her heart pounded and her hands turned ice cold.

'Dinner is ready, come and eat.' Lucie opened the door to Gerner's room where he was standing by his desk cleaning his nails.

He walked into the dining room and sat down at the table. In silence and without deigning to look at Lucie even once, he ate his soup. Lucie was in such anguish that finally she couldn't bear to hear the sound of her own spoon each time she lowered it to the bowl and lifted it to her mouth. She couldn't eat more than half of her soup.

'I met Mrs. Reinertson on the street today,' Lucie began, after Gerner had helped himself to the roast veal. 'She turned around and walked with me and insisted I come up to visit with her a while.'

Not a sound in reply.

The food swelled in Lucie's mouth and she was scarcely able to swallow it.

'I'm perfectly aware that you're angry with me, Theodor,' she said shyly after a while. 'I'll gladly apologise, if you want.'

Gerner wiped his mouth calmly and carefully, put the napkin down, stood up and left the room.

While Gerner took an after dinner nap in his room, Lucie stayed in the sitting room and listened for him to wake up.

Finally she heard him get up, and she quickly fetched the tray with coffee and carried it in to him. She usually drank coffee in his room with him, but today she had only set one cup next to the little silver pot. After she had poured his coffee, she went back into the sitting room.

Shortly afterward she heard Theodor go into the front hall and put on his coat.

'Oh God, he's going out without saying a word to me – what, what am I going to do! Is he really leaving, I wonder?' She strained to listen. 'Yes, he really is.

'Fine way to treat a person, I must say! – Mrs. Reinertson should know about this... He'll have a long wait before I play up to him again. – Ugh, he's so ugly when he's angry. – He scares me.'

Lucie found it unbearable at home that afternoon. She couldn't embroider, she couldn't read, she couldn't sit still anywhere. Oh, if only she could go see Mrs. Reinertson, unburden herself to her and then sit and listen to all the wonderful things she said. Her voice alone and her kind, shining eyes were a cure for all troubles. But it wouldn't do to go there twice in one day. Mrs. Reinertson had talked about being intrusive, but *that* would be intrusive.

Yet she wanted so badly to go out, just to pass the time and escape from all this unpleasantness. Wasn't there anyone in the whole city she could go visit? When she was at Tivoli she had never had any shortage of people to visit. – 'Nilsa,' she said out loud. 'What if I go and visit Nilsa?' It would be a solace and a relief to listen to her jabbering nonsense. – Then she could let herself imagine she was still at Tivoli and that everything was just like in the old days. – That would really be fun now that everything was so completely different. She actually longed to see Nilsen, to sit on the other side of a table that was piled with hat forms and cardboard boxes and feathers and trimmings, drinking coffee out of Nilsa's stoneware cups with the enormous roses, and dunking sugared rusks. Yes, that's what she'd do. Why shouldn't she do something to make poor Nilsa happy? When it took so little. Theodor would never have to find out.

VI
At Nilsen's

I'd better bring Nilsen the present I owe her for that bet, Lucie thought as she was walking down Karl Johan around five o'clock, all bundled up in a long fur cape and fur-trimmed rubber boots that she had pulled on over her shoes.

But what in the world should I get her?

'When you've got a fashionable hat and a pair of decent gloves,' she mimicked Nilsen. Gloves, of course! Then she won't have that expense for a while.

She went into a shop, bought the gloves, and quickly made her way down Øvre Slottsgate to the building next to the one where Theodor had his office. Hurrying through the entryway, she crossed a courtyard that was dimly lit by light from many windows, found the rear door and started up the narrow staircase, where a stale, acrid odour assaulted her. A lamp was hanging in the second-floor hallway, its tiny metal frame enclosing a piece of sooty glass. As she walked toward the stairs to the third floor, she passed several doorways and read by the dirty yellow lamplight:

Bernard Jensen, Typographer.

Oleus Schmidt, Master Tailor,
Men's clothing turned, altered, and repaired;
Stains removed.

Hansine Sørensen,
Gloves washed, feathers curled,
Silk ribbons re-dyed and restored.

There was no lamp on the third floor and Lucie had to grope her way forward until she came to a door. She knocked, heard the sound of water splashing and clothes being pounded in a washtub, and knocked louder.

Then there was the sound of wooden shoes, the door opened, and a wet, bare-armed woman appeared, enveloped in a cloud of grey, soapy-smelling steam that nearly filled the room. 'What do you want?' she asked.

'Would you kindly tell me if Miss Nilsen lives here?'

'Two people with that name live here,' the woman replied. 'One of them knits and the other one sews.'

'Does she sew hats?' Lucie asked. 'Because she's the one I want to see.'

The woman picked up a lamp, stepped into the hallway and pointed, 'Third door down. There's a sign on the door, too – she even had it printed.'

> *Miss Severine Nilsen,*
> Accepts orders for hats and accessories.

'Yes, here it is, sorry I bothered you,' Lucie nodded back at her.

There was a scraping of chair legs from inside when Lucie knocked at the door. 'Sit still, old boy, it's just a messenger coming to pick up a hat,' said Nilsen's voice, evidently nearing the door. The door opened and Lucie recognised the sour smell of tobacco.

'No, I don't believe my eyes! God, is it possible – Luciekins!' Nilsen looked red and flustered and stood in the middle of the doorway as if she were trying to hide something.

'I just wanted to deliver this,' Lucie said, handing her the package. 'Here you are. Wear them in good health.'

'Many, many thanks. I was only joking, you know. Oh, Lucie, Lucie!'

'Don't you ask people to come in, Nilsa?' said a voice from over by the window.

Lucie felt a little twinge go through her. Now she knew why this tobacco smell was so familiar.

'Yes, of course, please come in, Luciekins. I'm so surprised and happy I don't know what to do.'

'No, if you have company I won't disturb you,' said Lucie. She wanted to run away, but at the same time was irresistibly drawn to the tobacco smell that awakened so many strange memories.

'Oh, pooh, company,' Nilsen said with a forced laugh.

'We're old friends, after all,' said the voice, and at that moment Lucie saw two shirt sleeves and a soft, pallid face with a stiff black moustache, flashing eyes, and slicked-down hair above a square forehead.

Lucie pulled back with a start. 'Thank you, but I'll leave all the same. I don't want to intrude,' she said tentatively, without moving.

'That's what we get because you're sitting around in your shirt sleeves, Olsen,' Nilsen scolded. 'Of course we're old friends, but you should still have some manners. Come on now, Luciekins.' Nilsen pulled her across the threshold and shut the door.

'Put your jacket on, Olsen, I'll stand in front of you while you do it.' She picked up her skirt and held it out as far as the width allowed, nodding and giggling at Lucie. 'He lives in the building, you see, and drops in during the afternoon for a chat. But as a matter of fact, I've just told him I don't want him hanging around here any more. Hurry up, Olsen! Why don't you stand up?'

'It's not going to kill Lucia to see me in my shirtsleeves. Ha, ha, ha! I daresay it's a sight she's seen before.'

'Shame on you, Olsen, how vulgar you are.' Nilsen let go of her skirt, unfastened Lucie's cape and laid it on the tattered cover of her daybed. She picked up a rocking chair, its back missing several of the black-lacquered slats, and carried it over to the windows, where she set it down at an angle to the open game table. 'Sit down here, Luciekins, that's right. So Olsen can only see you from the side. That'll be his punishment.'

'Olsen can always move, you know,' said the man in the shirtsleeves, getting up from his chair by the window where he'd been sitting with his elbow propped on a corner of the table, smoking a pipe. He picked up his half-empty beer bottle and glass, walked past the table, around Lucie in the rocking chair, over to the other window and sat down.

'That's my seat, if you please! Get up this instant, Olsen! – God, a beer bottle right in the middle of my moiré ribbons!' Nilsen let out a yelp and held her hands protectively over her cardboard boxes and trimmings. 'You're ruining good money for me. Kindly leave the lamp where it is, old boy.'

'A man's got to be so damned careful with all these female accessories.' Olsen laughed good-naturedly, moving back to the daybed, and setting the bottle and the glass on the floor next to him. 'Anyway, I have a good view of Lucia from here, I do.'

'It's Mrs. Gerner, if you don't mind, isn't that right, Lucie?' said Nilsen as she put away the things on the table.

'Oh no, I think the other will do fine. What do you think, Lussia?' Olsen winked at Lucie, sliding his fingers inside his collarless neckband and casually scratching his neck.

'It's all the same to me,' Lucie answered with a toss of her head.

'Christ, I can easily call you Mrs. Gerner – I've certainly got nothing against that. Ha, ha, ha.' He bent down, poured beer into his glass and drank. Then he stood up, walked over to the windowsill and filled his now extinguished pipe from a cornet of Birdseye tobacco.

'You could button up your waistcoat, Olsen,' Nilsen said coaxingly. 'You ought to have that much respect for yourself, Olsen.'

'Why should I do that? It's so much more comfortable like this.'

'There's no getting anywhere with him.' Nilsen shook her head at Lucie as she carried the cardboard boxes, into which she had put her sewing things, over to the chest of drawers.

'Damn slippery out there again today,' Olsen said, after they'd been quiet for a bit.

'Yes, it's nearly impossible to go anywhere,' said Lucie.

'This morning an old woman fell and broke her leg,' Nilsen remarked.

Pause.

Then Olsen asked, 'Have you read *Albertine**, Lussia?'

'No, I have more respect for myself than that. Besides, Gerner says he won't have a book like that in his house.'

'I'm with Gerner. Why do they have to write those kinds of books?'

Another pause.

'By the way, Lussia, I have to tell you how glad I am to see you again,' Olsen said, reclaiming his previous position on the daybed. 'I think you're even more beautiful than you were before. I do believe my mouth is starting to water again.'

Lucie giggled.

'Don't answer him, Lucie, old girl,' Nilsen said. She'd finished clearing the table.

But Lucie was suddenly filled with a desire to be friendly and engaging. It was so very strange to see Olsen again, wearing exactly the same clothes as on those afternoons in the past, and she couldn't really understand why she had thought he was unpleasant and disgusting. He was an agreeable fellow, he truly was, and terribly amusing in fact.

'How are things going with you now, Lussia?'

'I'm just fine, thank you,' she replied animatedly. 'How about you?'

'I've never met such a great girl as you, my Lussia. It's such fun to see you again.'

Lucie giggled again.

'What a girl! Isn't that what I've always said?' Nilsen exclaimed. 'I've got to give you a kiss, Lucie, I do, I do, I do!' Nilsen leaned toward her, with her hands tucked between her knees.

'Enough of that kissing!' Olsen commanded. 'If any kissing needs to be done, I'll take care of it myself.'

'Now control yourself, Olsen old boy.' Nilsen straightened up and assumed an imperious expression. 'We'll have no dirty suggestions, if you please. – But I must look at what you brought me.' She picked up Lucie's package, which she had laid on the cupboard, and opened it.

'Gloves, wonderful, elegant gloves! Mmm,' she pressed them to her nose and inhaled the smell of leather. 'A brown pair, a grey pair and a black pair – three buttons! Oh, Luciekins, you're much too sweet, you truly are. Look, she knew exactly what I wanted. I want to treat you to a cup of coffee – may I? Please say yes! I have delicious thick cream and fresh Danish pastry – oh, say yes.'

'Thanks, I'd love to have coffee,' Lucie said.

'Little angel,' Nilsen fawned, throwing her a kiss. 'You'll treat us to a glass of cherry rum, won't you, Olsen?'

'More than one.'

Nilsen went over to the tile stove where a tin kettle was sputtering in the lower chamber. She took a coffee pot out of the cupboard.

'My feet are getting so warm,' Lucie said. 'I'd better take my boots off.' She put one foot in front of the other and started to push.

'Let me help you.' In a second Olsen was kneeling in front of her, his pipe in his mouth. 'Oh Lord, here's her innocent little footsie again.' Enraptured, he stopped and caressed her foot. 'And such fine soft shoes.'

'Ugh, you're so disgusting, Olsen.' Lucie giggled and tugged a little with her foot.

Nilsen had her back to them as she poured water into the coffee pot. Just then there was a knock and she went over to answer the door. A girl was delivering a hat along with a message about what should be done with it. Nilsen went out, shutting the door behind her.

Olsen put his pipe down.

'My sweet, sweet Lussia,' he said thickly, and taking a firm grip on her legs, slid his hands up and around, as far as her knees.

'Oh, but you're awful! Stop it, stop it, Olsen, or God help me, I'll scream,' Lucie said, trying to shove him away. But Olsen held her tightly and buried his face in her breast. 'Give me a kiss then, for old time's sake,' he said.

'Never in the world,' Lucie said, twisting herself to the side.

'Give me a kiss, or I'll take one by force,' whispered Olsen, lifting his face up towards hers.

'Will you let me go then?' Lucie asked.

'Yes, just give me one.'

Lucie bent down to him.

He let go of her legs, grabbed her waist and kissed her hard on the mouth as he pressed himself against her.

'My sweet child,' he said haltingly and out of breath. 'I've never cared for anyone as much as you, and I never will either. Nilsa makes a fuss over me, but I'd no more take up with that old bag of bones...'

49

The door latch clicked and Olsen quickly bent down and seized Lucie's other foot, which was still in a rubber boot. 'This one sure is hard to get off,' he marvelled, when Nilsen was back in the room.

'Something's going on in here,' Nilsen said sarcastically as she set cups and a plate of Danish pastry on the table.

'He's absolutely crazy, that Olsen,' Lucie laughed. 'On his knees all that time fumbling with these poor, innocent boots.'

'Oh, that fellow knows what he's doing,' Nilsen snapped. 'He's got all fronts covered.'

'I'll go get the cherry rum.' Olsen pulled on an old black coat that had been hanging over the back of a chair.

'Was he forward with you?' Nilsen asked after Olsen had left.

'No, he was just having a little fun.'

'Olsen always goes too far,' Nilsen said as she put the sugar bowl and the cream pitcher on the table. 'He lacks discretion.'

'Lord, it's so strange to be here with you and Olsen again!' Lucie cried, with a wriggling movement as if she were being tickled.

'Yes that's for sure. But the best thing is that you don't put on airs. That's really so nice of you.'

Olsen came back in and placed a bottle with a gaudy label and a red lacquered cork on the table. 'You'll have to provide the glasses, Nilsa.'

'A new one, how about that! There was a little bit left in the old one,' Nilsen said. 'He's in a generous mood today all right, ha, ha, ha!'

'Does she think we set half empty bottles out for company like this?' Olsen looked meaningfully at Lucie. 'That's fine when we're by ourselves, but not in this case.'

Olsen drank three cups of coffee and made sure the glasses were always full, especially his own. Nilsen's pale-grey cheeks gradually took on a hectic flush, and Lucie glowed and laughed non-stop, declaring that she was positively giddy from the rum, and that she hadn't had such a delightful evening since she'd been at Tivoli. Olsen's face got more and more sallow and his small grey-green eyes were watering and glassy.

Suddenly he bent his arm, placed his left hand on his shoulder, and moving his right arm back and forth as if he were playing a violin, started humming a dance melody.

'Yes, that's the one!' Lucie cried, jumping up. She picked up her skirts, lifted them above her ankles, and took some dance steps across the floor.

'Well, now we're going to have a real polka,' Olsen exclaimed, getting to his feet. He grabbed Lucie around the waist. 'Play the melody on a comb, Nilsa! You know it,' he hummed a few bars from a polka. 'It's too much to have to sing and dance at the same time.'

In a flash Nilsen had whipped out a comb, wrapped paper around it, and started blowing for all she was worth.

Olsen pressed Lucie tightly against him and danced across the sparsely furnished room, skipping and whirling around. Her feet scarcely touched the floor and her face often brushed against Olsen's cheek. Now and then she shrieked with laughter and cried for him to stop.

But Olsen danced on. It didn't bother him that Nilsen periodically dropped the comb in her lap to take a swig from her glass, laughing and pressing her hands to her stomach.

'How about a waltz!' he cried, standing still for a moment while he thought through the tempo. And then they went at it again until Nilsen cried out that by God her lungs were going to collapse.

'All right then, a gallop! Are you so old and decrepit that you can't keep going? Stay with it, Nilsa!' And Nilsen stayed with it until Lucie and Olsen literally rolled over onto the daybed, puffing like a bellows while the sweat rolled down their faces.

'Hahahaha, hahahaha! That's what I call a real dance,' laughed Olsen, holding his chest with both hands. Nilsen and Lucie chimed in until finally they sat gasping for breath, begging each other not to make them laugh any more.

After a while Lucie came to her senses and looked at the clock.

'God, it's already seven o'clock!' she exclaimed, alarmed. 'I've got to go home, right away!'

Olsen and Nilsen protested, but Lucie quickly put on her cape. She was worried that Theodor would get home before she did.

'Take it easy,' Olsen said. 'I'll walk you home, that goes without saying. A lady like you can't be out on the street alone, after all. I'll just go and get my coat.' Olsen hurried out.

'I'll come with you, too,' Nilsen said, picking up her coat.

When he returned, Olsen said in a displeased tone, 'Well now, so we're going to be three strong, that seems to be overdoing it.'

'I really need some fresh air,' Nilsen said.

As they walked down the stairs, Olsen took a firm hold of Lucie's wrist, slipped his index finger underneath the sleeve of her dress and moved it back and forth on her bare arm. 'I'll guide you,' he said. 'It's dangerous here if you don't know your way.'

Lucie suddenly felt so nauseated by him that she could have slapped his face and told him to go to the devil. But a kind of compassion or reluctance to break the mood kept her from showing her aversion. When they reached the second floor where the hanging metal lamp was still smoking, he pressed himself so tightly against her hip that he actually stepped on her toes.

Oh no, this is going too far, Tivoli-Olsen, Lucie thought to herself, wrenching her hand free, her face pale with indignation.

God, she's in love with me, Olsen said to himself. She's about to faint.

'Ugh, that lamp is so dirty and disgusting,' said Nilsen, who was walking in front of them. 'But it's better than nothing, I suppose.'

On the stairs leading down from the second floor Olsen put his arm around Lucie's waist and whispered close to her cheek, 'Will you meet me some evening, Lussia?'

This is what you get for coming down here, Lucie thought. She felt dizzy from the cherry rum and the dancing and passively let herself be led along. God, what if Theodor knew!

'Come, let me have your arm,' she said to Nilsen after they had walked across the courtyard, through the entryway and out onto the street.

'I want an arm, too,' Olsen said, taking hold of Lucie.

'Look here, Olsen, I don't want to be marched down the street like somebody under arrest.' Lucie pulled away.

Just as they were walking by the building where Gerner had his office, a tall, slim gentleman came out onto the street.

'Then you should let go of Nilsa and just walk with me,' Olsen said in a loud, insistent voice.

The gentleman, who was right in front of them, quickly turned around. The gleam from the nearby gas lantern caught one side of his face, and Lucie recognised her husband.

With lightening speed, she spun around and started fiddling with the clasp at the neck of her cape.

'Is there something I can help you with?' asked Olsen, putting his hand under her chin.

'Let me be,' she snapped and swatted Olsen across his fingers. 'That was my husband who just walked by; if he saw me, I'll be miserable forever.' Frightened, she turned her head toward Gerner. He was walking with measured steps a little way off.

'You two aren't walking with me,' she said, her eyes pinned on Gerner's back. 'Do you think I want to be seen on the street with the likes of you? Now that I'm a fine lady! You're such a slob, Olsen, and you, you gadabout!' She stamped her foot and her voice shook with contempt and anger. 'I'm running to meet my husband now. – You keep away from us, or he'll send the constable after you.' The words flew out of her mouth, and before Olsen and Nilsen could get over this unexpected change, she was far away down the street.

VII
Home Again

She saw her husband turn at the row of houses on the Grand Hotel side of the street and walk down the sidewalk. Quickly cutting across the street, she started running past the Parliament Building and Studenterlunden. The granulated snow flew up around her feet as she ran, heaving half-choked, wheezing breaths; her heart was pounding so hard she thought she would die. She had to get home before Theodor. At the beginning of Drammensveien she paused for a minute to catch her breath. Then she started to run again, taking small, hopping steps, until she reached her entryway on Incognitogaten.

Though she was sure she had arrived well before her husband, she was so frightened that her knees were shaking as she climbed the stairs. She waited outside her door for a bit, so she wouldn't be completely out of breath when Martine came to answer the bell.

'My husband hasn't come home, has he?' she said casually.

'No, madam.'

Quickly she took off her wraps and her rubber boots, lit the lamp in the sitting room, and picked up a book. But then she remembered that Theodor liked to see her doing needlework in the evening, so she took out a piece of embroidery.

About ten minutes passed before Gerner arrived. Lucie heard him go into the dining room and then his steps faded away.

'What if he still won't speak to me,' she thought, letting her work drop into her lap.

After a while he came back and went out into the front hall.

'Damn! I don't believe it!' Lucie stood up with her needlework in hand, rushed over and opened the door.

'Are you going out again, Theodor?'

'Yes.'

'Aren't you coming home for supper?'

'No.' He put on his hat, took his gloves out of his pocket, grabbed his walking stick and was gone.

She went back into the sitting room, stomped across the rug with clenched fists, and gave a little snort. 'Ugh, what a man,' she said out loud, flinging the embroidery with such force that it flew across the table into the corner sofa.

'Olsen – Christian – thank goodness for him. Rough, yes, but at least he's flesh and blood. He's got plenty to say and doesn't leave you sitting there like an old maid. – Now he's gone off in a rage about nothing. If you'd known about *that*… oh Lord, if you'd known about that. You'd have killed me, at the very least. – This is what I get for being faithful to him.'

'No thank you, I don't want anything,' she told the maid, who came to ask if madam wanted tea. She was completely stuffed from all those pastries. – That cherry rum had put her in such good spirits. It made her so happy that she didn't recognise herself. They didn't have any cherry rum in the house, but surely there was something else that was strong and good. By heaven, she was going to drink until she was tipsy. What else could she do to pass the time?

She went into the dining room, got out a bottle of Swedish punch, filled a glass and slowly emptied it in one gulp. – Oh yes, it was actually quite nice to be alone for a while. She poured herself another glass and drank it. 'Good and strong and sweet.' She licked her lips. 'Theodor has good punch. Dingelingeling for massa,' she hummed and went into the bedroom swinging her bustle.

'Dingelingeling for massa,' she sang as she found her bridal veil, a pair of light yellow silk stockings Theodor had given her, a Roman sash, some artificial flowers, and a short embroidered petticoat. She carried these things into the sitting room and laid them on an armchair in front of the tall, wide pier glass.

'Masquerade, queen of the night, flowing hair.' She loosened her hair and undressed.

'Lord, these stockings feel so wonderful.' She let her hands glide down over her lovely legs. 'Olsen would like these, ha, ha, ha.' She ran in her stocking feet to the buffet and drank more punch. When she returned, she put on the petticoat, and with a gold brooch, pinned the Roman sash to the right shoulder of the embroidered chemise and tied the ends together over her left hip.

> Nikola, Nikola,
> Ah, ah, ah!
> Nikola, Nikola,
> Ah, ah, ah!

she sang, looking at herself in the mirror and snapping her fingers. Then she gathered up her abundant golden hair, which reached all the way down past the split in her petticoat, and raising her arms so that her firm white breasts stuck out proudly, she fastened her hair at her neck with a red ribbon, poked flowers in on top and covered her head with the bridal veil, which fell like a white wave all the way down to her feet.

Smack, smack, she slapped her hips and sang:

> Clad in tight breeches and riding boots,
> Volte-Marche! Volte-Marche!
> All the ladies stop
> And stare.
> The pride of the cavalry!

'Oh Lord, oh Lord, Krohn was so darling when he sang that – I'll never ever forget him. And *Splendid* – he was sweet in that too.'

She fell silent, then burst into tears and stretched out her arms to her weeping image in the mirror. Yes, she was beautiful, oh Lord she was beautiful, but she had never seen it the way she did this evening. And that fool, Theodor. – Living here on Incognitogaten with a stuffy old man, like a slave or something. What kind of life is that for somebody who's been to London and Quebec with Mrs. Thorsen and her children? A silk dress for every day and a fur cape? She spat on it. No, seek your fortune out in the big wide world, carouse until you can't take it any more, and then marry a rich old man so you can be carefree in your old age. – Singelingeling for massa, singelingeling for massa . – Like Mrs. Reinertson says the fine ladies do, well, not carouse... no, how did that go? It was the men she meant. First they caroused until they were ready to drop, and then they married some innocent little thing. – What was the fun in that? Getting a person to be faithful to you who didn't know any better, but someone who had lived with other men and knew how different love could be, now that was something! That was just as good as getting a man to be faithful.

Theodor was so old now that it wasn't an issue. The road has at least been cleared of *one* prime impediment to happiness. What could she have meant by that? She mulled this over for a while, slightly unsteady on her feet.

'I think I've had too much to drink.' She lay down on the sofa, closed her eyes and felt herself sinking into a dizzy haze.

At midnight Gerner came home. When he saw that Lucie's bed was empty and had not been slept in, he went through all the rooms looking for her, and stood as though turned to stone, in front of the sofa on which Lucie lay. His eyes widened in astonishment, the upper part of his face seeming to swell and grow more prominent as the area around his mouth tightened.

Lucie was lying on her back with her lips slightly open, breathing deeply and regularly, her breast moving up and down under the thin chemise. An arm and one leg were hanging down toward the floor. The long golden hair concealed her shoulder and part of her dangling arm; the bridal veil spread across the floor. Gerner placed the lamp that he'd carried from the bedroom on the table.

'She's ravishing' – his expression softened – 'take her in your arms and carry her in to bed.' He stepped closer and bent over her, but then he remembered that he mustn't spoil the effect of the punishment for this morning's offence, and he quickly straightened up.

'So *this* is what she resorts to when she's bored. – Re-living memories of the old days.' – What in the world could he do to rid her of all these bad habits? It was certainly not as easy to educate her as he had imagined. He would have to keep a sharp eye on her at all times.

Hadn't she even tried to rebel against him with impudent retorts like the ones she made this morning? Indignation flared up in him. This must be treated with strictness, nipped in the bud; she must learn once and for all that such behaviour was not acceptable. Was *that* the gratitude she owed him? No, he begged her pardon, but he would not tolerate being corrected by *her*. She was going to feel what she had done. He would forgive her, to be sure, but not until she had been properly punished.

'And look at this place.' He cast his eyes around the sitting room. 'Straight out of the demi-monde.' Her corset was lying on the floor, her stockings were rolled up in a ball on the table, her dress was slung over the back of a chair and her petticoat had been tossed onto another. There were hairpins on the shelf beneath the mirror along with a comb and wisps of hair.

'Get up, Lucie,' he said sternly, 'and go to bed.'

Lucie leapt up, rubbed her eyes and made a hoarse throaty noise.

'If it weren't for the maid, I'd let you lie here, since this is the place you've chosen to sleep, but I won't have her finding you decked out like a dance-hall singer.'

Lucie looked around in confusion, and finally glanced down at herself. She had completely forgotten the way she was dressed, and when she realised how she looked, she bit her lip, hung her head, and curled up in the corner of the sofa as if to make herself smaller.

'See that you pick up your clothes and the comb and hairpins you've left lying all over the place,' Gerner said. 'I don't want you turning the sitting room into the backstage of Tivoli.' With that he picked up the lamp and left.

Lucie waited until she figured that he must be in bed. Then she silently crept into the bedroom. Gerner did not speak to her, and she quietly and carefully took off her clothes.

Both the following day and the day after that, Gerner stubbornly maintained his silence. Lucie was finally so tormented and miserable that she was beside herself.

On the evening of the second day, when Gerner came back from his office and went into his room, Lucie rushed toward him and threw herself down on the floor. She broke into loud sobs, begging and pleading for forgiveness for what she had said the other morning. She hadn't meant it, she knew very well how far above her he was – she was just a worthless little girl compared to him. It was bad and shameful of her to be naughty when he had been kind enough to want to correct her. Everything she was and had in the world, she owed to him. Oh she couldn't live unless he was gentle and kind to her; she had been so desperately unhappy these past two days – she'd received her punishment and it had been good for her, because not until now had she realised what a fine man he was and how badly she had behaved toward him.

Gerner looked down at the flat curve her body formed at his feet; she lay prostrate on her elbow and hip, her face covered with one hand, her shoulders jerking spasmodically with her vehement sobs.

'Get up, Lucie,' he said, after she had sobbed out what was in her heart. A tender smile on his lips, he bent over her, took hold of her waist, and pulled her up to his chest.

'There, there,' he whispered gently, and kissed her, crushing her against him. 'Now I recognise my old, sweet Lucie again.'

VIII
Nilsa

A month later, Gerner was walking home from the office one evening when he met Nilsen on the steps. Irritated, he had questioned Lucie, who rescued herself by making up a story that Nilsen had come to ask for money because she was on the verge of starving to death. Gerner was somewhat appeased when he learned that Nilsen had not come to see his wife in the capacity of a friend, but he firmly instructed Lucie that she should no longer receive her visits. If the woman was really as destitute as all that, she should write a letter instead. Afterwards it had occurred to him that it might be more proper for him to take the matter into his own hands and put an end to it. He had asked Lucie where Nilsen lived, but was told she had no idea, she'd forgotten to ask; whereupon Gerner resorted to the city registry.

The next morning, Nilsen was busy stitching a black lace hat, her hair uncombed and an old remnant of a Viennese shawl wrapped around her body. Occasionally she would lay the hat on the table to rub her thin, blue-veined hands and blow on her fingers. There was the sour smell of cold tobacco, for the stove had not been lit since the previous evening when Olson was there.

On the table among the cardboard boxes was a cup from which someone had drunk black coffee and a cracked plate with a half-eaten slice of sour bread thinly spread with hard white butter. Nilsen looked sad and tired. There were dark hollows in her cheeks and her thick lower lip was peeling and cracked.

'It's so dark today.' She moved closer to the window with her work.

'Brr, it's draughty in here.' She raised her head and looked across the courtyard at the grey stone wall of the front building; its high windows had curtained valences above and green shutters below, on which 'Warehouse' was written in large letters. She knotted the thread and with a squeaking noise pushed the needle in and out through the stiff hat form.

There was a knock at the door.

'Come in,' Nilsen said, looking up anxiously.

No doubt it was about the rent again.

'Might you be Miss Nilsen, herself?' asked a messenger boy, standing at the door with his cap in his hand.

'Yes old boy, that's me.'

'Here, I was supposed to give this to you,' said the messenger, stepping closer and putting a letter on the table.

'Who's it from?' Nilsen asked, as she eagerly examined the address.

'I don't know, but it was the lawyer who gave it to me. He said I was supposed to deliver it to Miss Nilsen in person, and now that you have it, goodbye.'

Nilsen's heart was pounding with curiosity and her frozen fingers trembled as she opened the letter. Inside were two crisp ten-*kroner* bills and a piece of paper with thick masculine handwriting.

'My word,' she said and began to read.

Miss Nilsen!

I beg you to accept the enclosed monetary token without any kind of misgivings. It is a pleasure for me to be able to extend this small helping hand, and you must not regard it as a gift but rather as a simple compensation for what you've done in the past for my present wife.

Should you get into difficulties in the future, I will still be willing to help you, of course within certain reasonable limits. But it is my firm desire, that you should not make overtures to my wife or in any way attempt to visit her at her home. My wife's altered circumstances make it desirable that she should not maintain acquaintances that date from a time both she and

I would do best to forget.

Hoping that you will honour my wish in this regard, I remain yours truly,

T.A. Gerner

'No, thanks – if he thinks he can buy me off...' Nilsen said indignantly, tossing the letter on the table. 'You've come to the wrong person this time, Mr. Gerner.'

'That is no offer for me, Sir Knight.' Nilsen crossed her arms over her breast and the Viennese shawl, drew herself up in the chair, and threw back her head:

> I may be poor and from humble stock,
> But my soul is as noble as yours,
> And a thousand times more pure.

'Really, these men, these men! Always on the prowl – yes by God, on the prowl.' She laughed with satisfaction. 'All because he saw me on the steps yesterday. I noticed him all right.' She nodded energetically. – 'His eyes actually flashed when he walked by me. – The first time I was up at Lucie's he got so flustered, yes by God, flustered! – One little sign and I could have left with him. But I've always been a such a considerate fool, I've only myself to thank.'

'How sly he is.' – Nilsen got up and walked around the room. 'Forbids me to go see Lucie any more so she won't notice anything – wants me all for himself – ha, ha!' Taking off her shawl, she positioned herself in front of the little oblong mirror in the worn gilt frame above the commode, took the hairpins out of her hair, undid the braids, and carefully combed her hair.

'And so tricky and smart, the way he wrote it. Nobody would know it's that kind of letter. But he'd better believe I see through him. I'll write a crushing answer – then he'll come in person to talk me into it. No, no Mr. Gerner! This will do you absolutely no good.' She turned toward the door, extended her arm and struck a pose. 'You love me, you say? – I'm not that kind of woman, go to your wife with your love. – What's that you say? You want to have me?' She gave a giddy squeal and rushed over to the window. 'You should have said that before, dear sir.' The words came proudly, accompanied by a dismissive movement of her arm. 'Now it's too late.'

She washed her face and hands, fastened her corset around her lank body, and put on her best dress. Then she fetched some paper from a drawer in the commode, took pen and ink, and began to write.

She wrote a two-page letter, but wasn't satisfied when she read it through. 'Better to be short and dignified,' she said taking a new sheet of paper.

To Mr. T.A. Gerner, Lawyer.
    I hereby return your money and regret the misunderstanding that has occurred. If fine gentlemen could someday learn that being poor and for sale aren't always the same, much would be gained.

Yours respectfully,
Severine Nilsen

She picked up the two ten-*kroner* bills to fold them inside the letter, and then began to think about them. God knows how long it had been since she had seen a ten-*kroner* bill. Think what she could get with this money. Her shoes were so worn out she couldn't wear them without galoshes, and now there were holes in the galoshes as well. Her feet got sopping wet in the snow and slush every day. And then she could buy some wood and coal. Nothing was as bad as sitting here freezing. If she spent five *kroner* for wood and coal, she could last until spring and then get herself a few summer clothes with the rest. She didn't have a thing to wear when there was sunshine, for she couldn't possibly wear her tattered old wool shawl much longer. No, it would be a sin to give the money away, absolute suicide. Instead she should take it as a sign that God was watching over her. Human beings were really just tools in God's hands, and it would be disrespectful to be proud. She took a new sheet and wrote:

To Mr. T.A. Gerner, Lawyer.
    Your letter and money have completely astonished me. I

don't understand what you intend by it, but I'll accept the money as a loan and pay it back as soon as possible. I'm doing that for one reason only, not to offend Lucie's husband. Please note, Mr. Gerner, that it's only in the capacity of Lucie's husband that I agree to have any dealings with you.

Yours respectfully and considerately,

Severine Nilsen

'Now of course he'll come and try to seduce me. It eggs them on when they get the cold shoulder,' she giggled as she folded the letter and slipped it into an envelope. 'But I know how to handle him. I won't make it easy, at least.'

When Gerner read her letter at the office before going home for dinner, the corners of his mouth twitched scornfully. 'What a vulgar creature,' he muttered, tearing the letter to bits and tossing them into the wastebasket.

IX
Before the Party

Two years had passed and the end of March was approaching.

Theodor and Lucie were going to the Mørks' house for dinner, and Lucie was dressed up and ready, waiting for Theodor to come back from his usual Sunday walk.

She was sitting on a low rocking chair, languidly pushing her foot against the carpet and making the chair rock slowly back and forth. Her cheeks were pale, the corners of her mouth were turned down, and her eyes stared indifferently ahead.

Today he wouldn't have to wait for her. So he wouldn't have *that* to complain about.

Anyhow she would rather stay home. To tell the truth, it was no fun going out with Theodor, because he sat and watched her, with those big, white, peering eyelids that saw everything, followed her into every corner, yes, even through walls and closed doors.

What a brute Theodor was. The way he gave her the silent treatment day after day, week after week, refusing to look at her, if she so much as answered him back or made a face when he nagged her. Like that time at the theatre last winter. Was it reasonable to act like she had committed some dreadful crime, just because she picked up an umbrella for an old man who was probably blind at the very least. Good Lord, what she had to put up with that time – just because she got annoyed and asked him if he really thought it was a criminal offence to pick up an old man's umbrella?

She thought his silences would drive her mad; it was like having a fever. And the way her heart pounded when she heard him coming home every day, or even when she was just sitting there waiting for him. She ended up thinking there were ghosts in the corners and black shadows slipping past her. And when he sat there without saying a word, it was as if the silence was roaring in her ears and filling her with terror, oh such terror that she felt like killing herself out of pure fright. And not until she crawled on her knees to him, pleaded and wept like an insane person, did he restore her to favour again. That's how it always was. Only then did her restore her to favour – Oh Lord, how he had broken her – he was strong, this fellow, and he didn't give in. Not if it killed him would he give in.

Now he had what he wanted; she was always on pins and needles now, so frightened of him that her whole body trembled whenever he looked at her. Now that he had educated her, he thought everything was just fine, for he was quite merciful and kind to her now. But if he only knew how angry and bitter she felt toward him. Sometimes she felt like she wanted to kill him just to get even. She wished to God she had never known or seen him.

She stood up, walked a few paces back and forth, and then sat down again. There wasn't a single person she could talk to. Not even Nilsa – now that she and Olsen had got married, Nilsa was as afraid of her as if she were the devil himself. And her relationship with Mrs. Reinertson had gone nowhere. She was always as sweet and pleasant as could be, but Lucie could never open up to her. It was as if something stood between them. And then she was shy with her. What always happened was that Mrs. Reinertson sat and talked while Lucie sat and listened, thinking what a lovely person she was, but not the kind she could confide in.

And she had not had a child. If she had, maybe Theodor would have behaved differently toward her, or at least he wouldn't have been able to criticise her for *that*. What a foul mood he had been in the times she thought she was going to have a baby and had misled him. As if she could help it. It was just the opposite, entirely his fault. She was very sure about that. But she'd be careful not to suggest that again. He had cured her once and for all of that. Ugh, how venomous he had been that time.

She was sick and tired of the whole business, even though she was only 23 years old. In ten years she would be 33, in twenty, 43, in thirty, 53 – 'How in the world am I going to live through all those years!' She drew herself up, covered her face with her hands, and leaned forward. Then she heard Theodor coming and leaped to her feet. She walked to the sewing table, took her work out of the basket and unfolded it with clumsy, careless fingers. When Theodor opened the door and asked if she was ready, she folded up her work, followed him into the hall and put on her coat.

X
At the Mørks'

Dinner was over, and the women were seated around a table in the sitting room drinking coffee.

Mrs. Mørk was talking about the difficulties she was having with her maids. The nursery maid had got up in the middle of the night to go to a dance, and the baby had screamed until he was blue in the face before they heard it in their bedroom.

'Oh these maids, these maids! And of course they break everything. If your purse was as deep as the ocean it still wouldn't be enough.' Mrs. Lunde was speaking. The wife of a sea captain, she had eight children and struggled mightily to get along on her monthly allowance.

And then they launched into stories about their housemaids' wastefulness and profligacy. When one flagged, the other started in.

Lucie listened with a stiff smile. None of the women turned to address her, but almost unconsciously left her out of the conversation. To remedy this painful situation, she feigned interest, shook her head frequently, and said at the right times, 'No, you don't say. How dreadful!'

The men strolled in from the smoking room; with glowing faces and smiling eyes, they seated themselves among the women.

A young fellow with red hands and flaxen hair combed into a stiff point over his forehead struck up a conversation with Lucie.

'Has madam gone to many balls this winter?' he asked.

'No, I'm afraid not. My husband doesn't care to dance, unfortunately.' Lucie smiled invitingly.

'Is that right?' the gentleman said, exposing all of his large, ugly teeth. 'He really should be obliged to, when he has such a young wife, don't you think? I suppose you weren't at the carnival either?'

'An outstanding likeness of Mrs. Mørk, don't you think?' Gerner came over to Lucie and handed her a photograph, while turning his back on the man with the teeth.

A slight shock went through Lucie. She had not seen Gerner come in with the others and thought he was still in the smoking room.

'Yes, it's a good likeness,' she said, eagerly looking at the photograph.

Gerner pulled a chair over to the table and sat down.

'Don't you think so, too?' In her confusion, Lucie reached behind her husband and handed the photograph to the gentleman, who stood there smiling like an idiot.

'Can't you leave that dolt alone?' Gerner whispered. 'Next you'll be asking him how many balls *he's* been to.'

'What do you say, Mrs. Gerner,' said Mrs. Mørk. 'Do you want to play cards or sit and talk?'

'My wife likes to play whist,' Gerner hurriedly replied.

'Have I done something wrong again?' Lucie muttered, looking anxiously at Theodor. 'He's Mrs. Mørk's brother, you know.'

'That shopkeeper,' Gerner answered savagely. 'Mrs. Mørk's brother, is *that* what you consider refined company? Yes, I'm coming now.' Mørk had called out that the table for ombre was ready in the smoking room.

'They're dancing at Mrs. Reinertson's,' Lucie said as she shuffled the cards, glancing up at the ceiling, which was actually shaking.

'Now, *there's* a widow who loves to entertain,' said Mrs. Mørk. 'It hasn't been a week since we were at a big party up there.'

'But we didn't dance then,' Lucie said with a sigh.

'No, but only the young people were invited tonight. There are loads of cousins in the family.'

'It seems a bit unusual for a widow to do that kind of thing,' opined Mrs. Lunde.

'Her brother, the pastor in Arendal, is very worldly too,' lisped a pregnant little assistant pastor's wife with heavy blue rings under her eyes. 'He's always scandalising the congregation, Jensen says.'

'And she defends *Albertine*,' Mrs. Lund went on. 'Well as I always say, if you don't have any children… I'm so pleased with my eight. I'd rather have 16 than none. Your lead, Mrs. Gerner.'

There was much more talking and gossiping than playing. Lucie tried to get into the conversation a couple of times, but wasn't successful. Feeling uncomfortable and out of place, she pretended to be intent on the cards. When it was finally time to eat supper she breathed a sigh of relief.

'I think that was the doorbell,' Mørk said. They had finished supper and were just getting up from the table.

'It must have been the street door,' his wife answered. 'But what in the world is that?'

They all paused, hands on their chairs, as they were moving them back from the table. Drifting in from the next room came an intermittent muffled clamour and the tones of a violin playing a march. Mrs. Mørk went over and opened the door. The others turned around quickly with a buzz of astonishment.

The sitting room was jammed with people wearing carnival costumes and masks on their faces. It was a gaudy mixture of knights and their ladies, peasants and Italian fishermen, gypsies and dancing girls. In front of them stood a fiddler dressed as a peasant and Mrs. Reinertson in a pale grey silk dress, a gold comb in her shiny brown hair.

'Well what do you think?' Mrs. Reinertson said laughingly to Mrs. Mørk, who had stopped in the doorway. She clapped her hands. 'My guests couldn't be restrained, they're simply wild tonight. First they scared the life out of me by coming in carnival costumes, and then they absolutely insisted on coming down here. You mustn't take offence.'

'How could you think that – what a fun idea they had. Come in, do come in.'

'Oh now you're shy,' Mrs. Reinertson laughed at her guests, who were clustered together with their arms linked, giggling in embarrassment and whispering behind their masks. 'What did I say?'

'How marvellous of you to come and liven us up.' With a bray of laughter, Mørk walked around shaking hands with the masked guests, who bowed and curtsied and made somewhat fruitless attempts to be amusing.

'Now make yourselves at home and *act* your parts to your heart's content. By heaven, we'll have champagne! Here Lina.' He handed a ring of keys through the dining room door.

'Now really Aksel,' said his wife angrily, snatching the keys away from him. 'The maids in the wine cellar...'

'Look, Mrs. Lund!' Lucie was so excited that she impulsively took Mrs. Lund's arm and pointed at a harlequin who was walking on his hands among the armchairs. 'Oh Lord, oh Lord, the lamp!' she cried, clinging tightly to her arm. The harlequin's feet were close to a porcelain lamp on a little marble table.

With a strained expression, Mrs. Lund moved away from Lucie. 'A bit common, don't you think,' she said to the assistant pastor's wife, taking her by the arm.

Champagne corks were going off explosively in the dining room and Mørk poured. 'If you please, ladies and gentlemen!' he called. 'People who want champagne must come in here!'

'But first take off your masks!' said Mrs. Reinertson with a clap of her hands, after which they all took off their masks and let them dangle from their arms. Then they began to laugh and talk, recognise and introduce themselves, as they all crowded around the table in the dining room to drink champagne.

There were speeches and toasts, and gradually the somewhat forced animation that had covered embarrassment gave way to a rush of good cheer.

Lucie was looking through narrowed eyes at a good-looking young man, tall and broad-shouldered, with a black moustache, red lips, and gleaming healthy teeth. He was wearing sandals on his feet and a monk's cowl over his lieutenant's uniform.

'Your health, madam,' he said clinking his glass against Lucie's. 'Long live celibacy!'

'Long live what?' Lucie asked, laughing heartily. 'I don't know what you mean.'

'You are adorable, madam!' The lieutenant threw back his head and gazed at her rapturously with brown, laughing eyes. 'Should I explain it to you? Oh no, I would rather explain what celibacy is *not*. We'll take our glasses with us.' He offered her his arm.

'Don't be such a flirt, Knut,' Mrs. Reinertson whispered in his ear, as he and Lucie walked by. 'Her husband is so jealous.'

'Then we'd better cure him,' Knut replied. 'She's so sweet and amusing, Aunt.'

'Let's sit over here.' The lieutenant led Lucie to a little sofa in a corner of the sitting room beneath a tall arrangement of leafy plants, and sat down beside her. He began to chat with her in a soft, confiding tone.

Gerner observed them from the dining room, where he was talking to a knight's lady dressed in black velvet with a tall mother of pearl comb in her hair. He watched Lucie laugh and drink champagne. Occasionally she would lean back and lift her feet off the floor. Once she turned away, as if her admirer had been too forward, and the lieutenant gave her a surprised look and became earnest and intense. Gerner's half-shut eyes were narrowed more than usual and his nostrils twitched nervously.

'What are you staring at?' the knight's lady asked, turning around.

'That monk over there is amusing.' – Gerner forced his mouth into a smile. – 'That fop of a lieutenant in the monk's cowl.'

'Oh Knut Reinertson. Knut Lionheart.'

'Oh yes? Why do they call him that,' Gerner interrupted.

'I don't know really, but I suppose it's because he's a heartbreaker. – Who is the lady he's talking to?'

'It's my wife,' answered Gerner, looking at the knight's lady with his eyes wide open.

'Oh I see – well I'm sure we were introduced but I didn't hear the name. She is really very charming. – If only he doesn't hypnotise her.'

'Hypnotise?'

'Yes, didn't you hear about that? It's quite dreadful the things he gets people to do and say. At a party the other night – papa wouldn't give me permission to try it. – What! Go up to Mrs. Reinertson's and dance? – Oh yes, let's do that!' She clapped her hands.

'What do our guests say?' cried Mrs. Mørk looking over at her husband.

'Let's go up, go up,' they all answered.

'Let me lead the way,' Mrs. Reinertson said, taking the fiddler by the arm.

'That's what I call hospitable,' Mørk exclaimed, offering Mrs. Lund his arm.

Gerner wanted to reach Lucie to tell her they should go home, but he couldn't get past all the people and furniture. He stretched sideways over the others' shoulders in order to catch her glance, but she pretended not to notice.

'Devil take it,' Gerner mumbled, when he saw her follow the others out the door, flushed and laughing on the lieutenant's arm.

'Tonight I intend to enjoy myself,' Lucie said to her escort, lifting her knees in a little dance. 'It's certainly been a long time. – Imagine, I haven't gone dancing one single time since I got married.'

I don't care if he kills me, I'm having a good time tonight, she thought. There'll be a scene anyway, might as well get some fun out of it.

'Do you not have a partner, Gerner?' asked Mrs. Mørk. 'Then you'll have to be content with me.'

He bowed silently and they left the room.

From the entryway he saw Lucie and the lieutenant turning into the bend of the staircase that led to Mrs. Reinertson's apartment. They were close together. His head was bent toward Lucie's and she was looking up at his face as he spoke.

Mrs. Mørk chattered on and on, but Gerner heard nothing; he just stared up the stairs with a white face and clenched lips.

'I wish I had a sixth sense,' said the lieutenant.

'Oh, and why is that?' Lucie asked.

'So I could look into your soul and read my fate.' His face was mirthful but his voice was solemn.

'Oh you,' Lucie laughed, poking him in the side with her elbow.

'Every young woman's heart is an unsolved riddle, a boundless deep – an ocean of – in a word – riches and possibilities – oh, a bottomless. . .' he paused for a moment. 'It's a sin to keep such a treasure locked away.'

Lord, he's sweet, and it's so poetic, the way he talks, Lucie thought, her face alight with rapture. And he's such a gentleman.

'Oh I think you'd soon have your fill of that treasure, I do, Lieutenant Reinertson.' Her voice was trembling with delight and agitation.

'Try me, madam,' he begged earnestly. 'Tell me what you are thinking, feeling, what delights you, makes you suffer' – he softly squeezed her arm – 'especially suffer, for is there any human being who doesn't suffer?' – They had now come upstairs into rooms lit by candelabras and lamps, where the musician struck up a waltz.

And then the dancing couples whirled down the large, rectangular dining room.

Reinertson clasped Lucie firmly to his chest and danced off. She closed her eyes and leaned back against his arm. Never before had dancing felt so delicious. She felt like she was flying through the air and that her body was almost dissolving in a wonderful, tingling sensation. The furniture, the people, and everything else drifted away. She was conscious only of him and herself, and, from far away, the sound of the music. If only it never, never had to end.

'I'd surrender my soul to the pains of Hell for the key to her rooms,' the lieutenant whispered after the dance, when they were sitting in an alcove off the dining room.

Blood pounded in Lucie's ears. She leaned back, fanning herself with her handkerchief. A soft smile trembled at the corners of her mouth, and her breast rose and fell. 'Oh, if only I had met you before, Reinertson,' she whispered back, and squeezed his hand.

This is getting amusing. She thinks I'm in love with her, thought the lieutenant.

'We can still get to know each other, of course,' he said softly, squeezing her hand in return. Rubbish, I can't be bothered with this, he thought a second later, just as Lucie was about to answer. He released her hand and said, 'Come, let's dance the gallop together.'

They stood up and Lucie took his arm.

In the doorway, they met Gerner.

'Well here you are, finally,' he said. 'It's time to go home.'

Lucie could tell from his voice how much it was costing him to control himself. But she didn't feel the slightest trace of fear, only a boundless joy that she was going to dance with *him* again.

'Just a couple of times around, counsellor,' said Reinertson, 'then I'll return her to you.'

He danced off with her. Gerner watched them.

'Now I'll take my leave and surrender your wife to the hands of her natural guardian, as they say.' The lieutenant had brought Lucie back to Gerner. 'Goodnight, madam. Thank you for this evening. Goodnight, counsellor.' He bowed and left.

Lucie's eyes followed him through the room with a longing expression. She seemed to have completely forgotten that Gerner was standing beside her.

'Do you hear, we're leaving.' He grabbed her firmly by the wrist and walked toward the door.

'I should say goodbye first, don't you think?' Lucie tried to free her hand.

He tightened his grip and actually pulled her past the dancing couples. 'You're coming now!'

'Leave without thanking them?' Lucie said sharply, out in the front hall.

'Don't try to prolong the scandal.' Gerner opened the door and pushed Lucie out through it. He could barely get his words out and his hands were shaking.

I don't care if he's in a good mood or a rotten mood, Lucie thought, as they were walking down the stairs. As long as I can see that darling Reinertson again soon.

But when they were putting on their coats in the Mørks' well-lit front hall, the sight of Theodor's pallid cheeks and clenched lips sent a chill through Lucie.

Striding down the street, Theodor took such long steps that Lucie had to trot to keep up with him. Finally she slowed and trailed along behind.

'Is it your intention to play the part of a streetwalker tonight?' Gerner had stopped by the university to wait for Lucie.

'How can anybody keep up when you run like that,' Lucie answered angrily and walked past him.

'You are to conduct yourself properly.' In a couple of steps Gerner was beside her. 'Reminding everybody of what a trollop I married.' His voice was distorted with rage.

'You're really so crude,' Lucie said indifferently, walking hurriedly, almost running.

'If a man so much as looks at you, your whole body starts to tremble,' Gerner went on, getting more and more agitated. 'You make me look ridiculous.'

'Well, that's not difficult, is it,' she said with a scornful breath.

Gerner could have hit her.

'You be careful,' he snarled. 'You're a tart, and you'll never get that out of your blood.'

'A tart! I really have to laugh. You should hear what Mrs. Reinertson has to say. I suppose you were lily-white when you married me.'

'Now you start with impertinences – you've wisely refrained from that until now.'

'But I won't stand for you treating me this way any more.' She spoke breathlessly because of their quick pace on the slippery snow. 'I won't stand for it any longer, just so you know. I suppose you think being married to you is so glorious!'

'Be quiet!' He grabbed her shoulders and shook her so violently that her little fur hat flew off her head. They had turned onto Drammensveien, and he gave her a shove that propelled her a few steps along the street.

Without uttering a sound, Lucie bent over to retrieve her hat, then took off down Drammensveien with her hat in her hand, as if she were running for her life.

XI
During the Night

Gerner neither slowed nor quickened his steps when Lucie dashed away from him. 'If you thought you'd scare me, you figured wrong,' he muttered. 'Who but a tart would do such a thing? Running off in the middle of the night.'

When he turned into Incognitogaten she had long been out of sight. He calmly walked on, steadied by his walking stick, and soon arrived at his building. He closed the street door without locking it, climbed the stairs, and left the front hall door ajar. Then he went into his room, lit the lamp, and paced back and forth across the room, his hands clasped behind his back and his head bowed.

He was filled with rage at Lucie and pity for himself. This frivolous tart that he had lifted out of filth and made his wife was setting herself against him. A woman who ought to be imbued with one single thought, one single goal: to erase the past, to be eternally on guard to show him she had become a different person, to show him that not one drop of her blood yearned for anybody but him, *desired* anybody but him. She ought to be humble and repentant, a penitential Magdalene in mind and deportment. *Then* everything would be fine between them, because he really was in love with her, yes, that was what made it so painful, he was still in love with her.

But how did she conduct herself? Oh, her smile and her expression as she was listening to that fop tonight. Exactly the same way she used to receive his advances, and the way she had received those of the others before him. It was enough to drive him mad. Everybody, everybody must of course see her past written all over her. That's why the men were so forward. With proper ladies their behaviour was quite different. He had noticed it again and again, for in truth, he had done little but pay attention to such things since his marriage.

And the way she constantly shocked and provoked him. Like the other day when Mørk was talking about the Swedish singer who had men going in and out of her window at night. The hearty way she laughed, and the expression on her face! As if she were wallowing in the memories! And then to tell him afterwards that it was so Mørk wouldn't think she'd been reminded of herself.

Not a trace of regret or disgust about her previous life. – Not a trace.

Only yesterday morning she was reading out loud from the newspaper about seduced girls, secret births, and prostitution! Instead of doing her utmost to avoid every reference to such things. He felt, each time, as if she were plunging a knife in his heart.

Gerner struck his forehead and groaned out loud.

'She has no conception of what I suffer. She utterly lacks the ability to comprehend it.

'And then she makes a scene about the way I treat her and says she won't put up with it. She should know how often I restrain myself and what it costs me. She should know the poison that's in my blood, how the struggle between these different feelings is tearing me apart; my moods swing from one minute to the next between pleasure and disgust, happiness and anger, love and repulsion. The thought of the other men who've had her always comes between us, hangs over me like a nightmare, turns my heart hard and cold, and the slightest provocation is enough to overwhelm me and smother every bit of happiness.

'Whenever I see a woman approached by a man on the street, I instantly think of her. Or if one of those sluts tugs at my arm, or I read a book, see a play, or hear a song. – The poison is inside me and around me – in *everything* and every place. And I'll never be able to overcome it, never, not as long as I live.'

He settled himself deeply in an easy chair and stretched out his legs.

'Well, things were different then,' he said with a heavy sigh. His eyes had come to rest on a photograph on his desk; it was of Lucie, taken the day before their wedding.

'What a fool I was!' He suddenly leaped to his feet and began to pace the floor again. 'You don't erase a past like that. Nothing can be erased. Everything, everything is subject to the law of necessity.

'Imagine if she had never belonged to anyone but me' – he raised his clenched fists and then lowered them – 'I could have been so happy, oh so happy.

'How did I get so entangled with her?' He had stopped beside his desk, picked up her picture, and was looking at it.

'Ah, that velvety skin' – his mouth had taken on a tender, almost child-like expression – 'and the promise in those smiling eyes.

'How did it happen?' – He set the picture down.

'What is it that binds a man to a woman, so that he can't follow any path except towards her, even if he wants to? Maybe it's just a couple of ringlets at the nape of her neck that your eyes keep returning to again and again, as if drawn by a magnet, or the little dimple that you can't take your eyes off, or maybe it's something else entirely. – I have no idea.

'They become chains – tough, unbreakable chains.

'Suppose I hadn't married her – a poor life perhaps, but at least a free man, without all this gnawing misery. And yet – I *can't* give her up, not divorce her. But wish I'd never laid eyes on her? – I'd give years of my life for that.

'What kind of life are we living?' He stopped in the middle of the room. 'I'm pacing round here like a hunted animal, and she...' He pulled his watch out of his pocket.

'My God – almost four o'clock! Well, there won't be many people out on the streets. The only ones out there should be the police.

'What if she's been accosted by someone? – What if she's gone off with him just to get even with me? Oh no, no, you wretch!' He slammed his foot on the floor.

'Scoundrel!

'How dare you think such base thoughts about her – about Lucie, your wife who loves you – because she does love you, and she's pure and good in spite of everything, and you *know* that, and still you keep hounding her the way you do. Oh what a miserable creature I am!' He covered his face with his hands and in a tearful, broken voice went on in a whisper, 'If only my grief could turn her past into lies and my love could make her pure and innocent – and once that was done, if I could feel the rapture of her embraces just once, for just a short time, without these disgusting, painful memories coming between us.'

His tears streamed down and wet his fingers; he took out his handkerchief and dried himself.

'If I had the courage, I'd put a bullet in my head and free her from the torment and misery in her life. Because that's what I *am*.

'Torment and misery.' He waved his hand. 'She's bold and daring enough. That's plain from what she had the nerve to throw in your face tonight. She's like a spring that jumps back whenever you push it down.

'Infernal warm, soft, downy skin – and then the way her body comes trembling to life.' A smile flickered in the corners of his mouth, and, slowly, as if in a dream, he paced the floor.

But why didn't she come? Where was she? Once before she had run away from him on the street at night, but then she had come home after half an hour.

– Well, he had gone too far with her tonight. She hadn't really done anything but dance and talk, and that was what everybody else was doing. But what was the use. He had sworn a solemn oath so many times that he would be governed by reason, but he had learned to recognise his impotence. He made no more promises. There was nothing to be done about it. He must continue to torture her, must continue to suffer. He was a man accursed. Nothing but the death of one of them could bring relief and liberation.

But where in the world was she?

He walked over and opened the window, then peered down at the street.

No one in sight.

At that moment he heard someone on the stairs. Quickly he closed the window, blew out the lamp and hurried into the bedroom. She mustn't know that he had been worried about her. Quickly he undressed, got into bed, and pulled the covers up over his shoulders, all the while straining to hear her footsteps.

'She's creeping into the sitting room to sleep on the sofa, like she's done before when we've had a fight,' he thought, when everything remained still. 'As long as she doesn't sleep so late that Martine finds her. I'd better check on that.'

Shortly afterwards he fell into a deep sleep.

XII
In the Morning

When he woke up at eight o'clock, he saw that Lucie's bed was empty and undisturbed.

With a start, he jumped out of bed, thrust his feet into a pair of slippers, threw on his dressing gown and went into the sitting room.

She wasn't there.

Out in the front hall the door was still standing ajar, and her coat wasn't there.

A terrible fear rose in him. He staggered and his heart seemed to stop beating.

Like a sleepwalker he returned to the bedroom, washed and dressed himself, and once again walked through the rooms looking for her in corners and behind the furniture, as if searching for a package he had lost.

In the dining room where the coffee table was set, he wandered slowly and aimlessly from place to place. One moment he was at the window looking down at the street, a moment later he was standing in the middle of the room.

Then he heard a rustle in the front hall, and immediately afterwards the dining room door opened; Lucie entered and walked across the room. She was dreadfully pale; there were bluish streaks on her cheeks and her eyes were swollen. Her hair was dishevelled and her face blank.

When she spotted Theodor, she stopped, clenched her fists threateningly, and choked out some words that were unintelligible. Then she hurried into the bedroom and quickly undressed. She dipped a towel in water and wrapped it around her face and head, then pulled on a night-gown and crept into bed.

The door opened and her husband leaned over her. She closed her eyes more tightly and lay quite still.

'Where were you last night, Lucie?'

She turned her head away from him carefully, as if it hurt her to move, and pressed her face against the pillow.

'How could you behave like that, Lucie? You're as uncontrollable as a wild animal when you're angry.'

No reply.

'For heaven's sake, you've got to be more careful, Lucie. It's going to end in disaster. A man can't calmly look on while his wife disgraces herself.'

'Can't you leave me in peace!' Lucie almost screamed, pressing her face into the pillow again, her shoulders tightening convulsively.

'You owe me an explanation of where you were and what you were doing.'

'I walked and walked,' she said impatiently, kicking her feet under the covers.

'For all those hours?'

'Yes, I sat down on the edge of the road to rest and fell asleep! And then I walked home. Can't you leave me in peace!'

'And nobody spoke to you?'

'No, of course not.'

'You didn't meet anybody!'

'No, of course not. Can't you leave me in peace!'

'I would like you to realise…'

'My head is going to burst if you say another word,' Lucie shouted, beating her heels against the mattress so that the bed shook. 'Get away from me! Go! Can't you see how sick I am!'

It's useless trying to talk sense to her now, Gerner thought, straightening up. I'll have to wait for another time.

'Shall I ask Martine to look in on you?' he asked, with his hand on the door handle. 'I'm going to the office now.'

'No, just leave me in peace!'

'Don't you want some coffee or something to eat?'

'No, just peace! I've got to sleep or I'll die.'

– – – –

Oh yes, sleep.

Oh if only she could sleep one hour and get rid of this pounding headache.

Don't think about it – Just don't think about it.

Never mind, it wasn't really so terrible as long as nobody knew it happened.

But if she were a fine lady, one of those who had never been with anybody except her husband, she probably would have killed herself after this.

Oh, if Theodor knew.

She had been so determined to tell him about it, look him right in the face and say she'd been raped out in the fields by a horrible, dirty fellow in filthy work clothes, so Theodor would see what came of treating her like he did. But as soon as she got a glimpse of that impassive face and those white, self-righteous eyelids, her throat closed up and her tongue felt thick in her mouth.

And yet she had been looking forward to telling Theodor about it. That was what had given her courage to come home, for otherwise she would never have dared to show herself again after the way she had talked back to him on the street last night.

But now – not if she were going to be burned alive could she tell him.

'Ugh, what a brute,' she shuddered and covered her face with her hands.

'Lie still, lie still! If you scream I'll kill you' – Oh she could hear his hoarse, gasping voice, feel the revolting stink of him.

She tossed the blanket aside, swung her feet to the floor, and pulled off her nightgown and thin woolen undershirt. Taking the soap dish from the washstand she went into the alcove where there was a half-filled bathtub. She sat down in it and washed her entire body with soap.

A short time later she lay down on the pillow again and tried to sleep.

Big shiny tears trickled from under the long eyelashes and rolled slowly down her cheeks.

Oh God, life was so different from what you imagined.

At every turn in the road.

It wasn't only that being married and a fine lady were different than what she expected. But what you wanted most never happened, and what you didn't want did happen.

Like last night.

If only she hadn't climbed over the fence and lain down on that hill under the tree where the snow was almost gone – could she possibly find that place again, where she had climbed over the fence? It was definitely way past Skarpsno, almost out to Sandviken, because it seemed like she had walked for miles. The tree with the large bare drooping branches, she would know it the moment she saw it.

Oh, if only she hadn't climbed over the fence. She hadn't been all that tired, it was just to make the time pass, maybe fall asleep and catch a fatal illness, for it was dangerous to sleep on the ground, considering how sweaty she was. That would have served Theodor right. Or some robbers might have come along and taken her fur coat and watch and gold jewellery and choked her to death to keep her from screaming. – Then Theodor would have read about it in the newspaper. Found, the body of a lady – the people who found her could tell she wasn't a common girl because they'd probably have let her keep her expensive embroidered slip, and also the long, tight stockings that were so hard to take off.

If only she hadn't climbed over the fence. Or if she hadn't had that dream about Lieutenant Reinertson – oh that lovely, false dream – then she could have put up a fight in time and maybe saved herself. He was looking at her so sweetly, so tenderly in the dream – he was bending over her, and lying down close to her. And she felt like she was lying on a bed with soft silken blankets and sheets of dazzling-white lace. But then the weight on her breast got so heavy that she woke up, and there was somebody breathing in her face, reeking of tobacco and brandy. Oh Lord, oh Lord. She wrung her hands.

That dark male face and stiff, bristly beard, the wild eyes that were bulging down at her, the wet, gaping mouth, and the huge brown hairy birthmark on his cheek, right under his left eye. Oh that birthmark, that birthmark! It was almost the worst thing of all.

She sat up in bed and pressed her knees to her chest.

She had sat the same way, staring after him when he ran away, until she was so stiff that she thought she wouldn't be able to move her legs when she stood up. The terrible stink still clung to her coat.

Well, that was life. She had been dreaming about the sweet lieutenant and got a common labourer, maybe even a jailbird or an arsonist who'd escaped.

'Lord, my head is splitting!' She lay back down on the pillow. 'I'm so sick and tired and angry.'

'If only I can see Lieutenant Reinertson again soon.'

'Such a gentleman! The way he looks at you – and the way he talks!'

Maybe she would meet him on the street. He'd surely come over to greet her, and walk down Karl Johan with her, the way fine gentlemen did with fine ladies.

And it was so obvious that he was in love with her.

Oh, the way she would feel with *him* walking beside her. People would turn around and say: 'There goes Mrs. Gerner with her lover.'

Get rid of this headache, so she could go out for a walk in her new long winter coat and her muff with the silk bow and her flattering grey veil.

But first she had to sleep, that was the most important thing, or she wouldn't even be able to keep her eyes open.

Her head ached so.

XIII
Summertime

Summer arrived, bringing very hot and humid weather.

The earliest Gerner would be able to have his vacation was late in August. His plan was to take a trip with Lucie to a spa up in Gausdal.

There had been some discussion about renting a place in the country, and Lucie had found a little cottage that was suitable on Malmø Island, near Mrs. Reinertson's house. But at the last minute, Gerner had changed his mind and said he couldn't afford it. The real reason was that he didn't like the idea of Lucie spending so much time with Mrs. Reinertson, for he had a vague sense that in some way or other she egged Lucie on.

Mrs. Reinertson had invited Lucie to come out and spend a week with her on Malmø.

Lucie was not feeling well. She was often plagued with nausea and headaches. Her face had lost its freshness and the hollows in her cheeks had deepened.

She was in a painful state of uncertainty about whether or not she was pregnant, but continued to hope that it wasn't true.

Because if it *was* true, she was sure it was because of that night out in the field.

And that would be too horrible.

She often wondered why Theodor didn't ask her about it.

But she figured he had gotten so used to waiting and hoping, that it wouldn't even occur to him.

And she certainly wasn't going to say anything. She'd be careful about that, all right.

How strange that he didn't suspect anything, now when it actually might be true.

Oh no – she couldn't possibly be.

She's so dull and apathetic these days, Theodor thought, as he paced back and forth in his room. I can't get a word out of her. It's that ill-bred defiance in a new form.

Accompanied by Mørk, they had made an excursion out to Bygdø, where they walked in the forest, had supper in the Swiss Hut, and came back on the train. Mørk had scarcely left them before Lucie was informed that she'd behaved improperly by turning to look at a man kissing a trollop on a bench outside Frederiksberg Garden.

Now Lucie was standing by the open window, looking out at the warm, still summer evening, while Theodor walked slowly back and forth issuing reproaches, which she had no inclination to hear and therefore didn't hear.

She was thinking that it must be because she was looking so pale and wan these days that Lieutenant Reinertson hadn't come over to talk to her in the street, instead of bowing to her in that stiff, distant way. If he only knew how taken with him she was. He'd surely come then, even though she wasn't as strikingly beautiful as before.

'I'd be obliged if you would take the trouble to answer me,' Gerner said, stopping behind her after some moments of silence.

'I thought you preferred me to be silent,' Lucie said dully. 'You can't bear it when I talk back to you.'

'There are many ways to be silent. If you just looked the slightest bit – I won't say apologetic, but as if you even noticed what I said.'

If she went to see Mrs. Reinertson, perhaps she would meet the Lieutenant there, Lucie thought.

'Now admit that you behaved badly out there, Lucie.' Theodor took one of her limp hands.

She turned her head in his direction and gazed absently past him.

'I *am* right, isn't that so, Lucie.'

'Right, about what? I don't know what you're talking about.' She turned her head again and stared out the window.

He violently slung her hand away and walked quickly through the rooms into the bedroom.

'What a hothead,' Lucie said with a scornful laugh.

'I'd better sleep on the sofa tonight. I can't be bothered to go in there with him.' She began to unbutton her dress and walked into the sitting room where she arranged a velvet pillow and afghan on the sofa. As she turned to go over to the mirror to undo her hair, she saw a letter lying on the writing desk.

It was from Mrs. Reinertson, who was writing to say that she hoped Lucie would soon keep her promise to visit her on Malmø; in two weeks she was leaving on a trip with her sister Henny Brandt, who had come home from Paris and was living with her now. Gerner could come out and see them afternoons when he finished at the office, if he felt like it, and he could stay overnight from Saturday until Monday. It was just too sad to remain in the city in this heat, especially for Lucie, who ought to be staying out in the country.

'I'll go out tomorrow on the eleven o'clock boat,' Lucie exclaimed. 'Yes, by God, as Nilsa would say. I won't tell Theodor anything, because he'll just say no. And I *am* going out there.'

XIV
On Malmø

'Has Fredrik gone for a swim?'

'Yes, I think so.'

Henny and Mrs. Reinertson were sitting in a little summerhouse constructed like a grotto at the right of a large, dark-timbered house built in the Norwegian-Swiss style. The house lay high above the fjord on a steeply sloping hill, which was terraced all the way down to the white gravel road by the steamship wharf.

Both women were wearing light housecoats, and Henny's hair, still moist after her swim, hung loosely down her back. Mrs. Reinertson was holding a piece of crochet work in her hands, which were resting in her lap, and through the summerhouse door she gazed at the fjord, so bright and unmoving in the white sunshine that it seemed glazed with ice.

'Look at the ships and boats, Henny,' Mrs. Reinertson said. 'Isn't it striking the way they look like they're stuck in the ice, and yet they're moving? I've never seen anything so strange.'

'It must be the heat, and because it's so dead calm,' answered Henny. 'Fredrik seems sad, Karen.'

'Yes, the poor thing. He's proposed marriage and been turned down.'

'He told you that?' Henny looked at Karen in surprise.

'No, but I can tell in other ways. The last time he was in town two years ago, he went around the whole time singing to himself:

> You ask who she favours, and if she is fair,
> The woman I've chosen for my bride.

'Now it's a sad song from *Gluntarne** about blasted hopes and the

90

vanity of the world. I'm sure it's that Hilda Holm in Arendal who's engaged to marry Marstrand.'

'I can understand why she wouldn't accept him. If only he weren't a pastor.'

'No, he's not at all suited to it,' said Karen. 'But surely he must be able to find himself a wife.'

'Is he staying here awhile?'

'No, he's going up to Grefsen this afternoon.'

Henny removed the newspaper wrappings from a pair of shoes that been repaired in the city and that the housemaid had picked up that morning.

The steamship whistle reverberated up to them, doubly strident and piercing in the still, sun-drenched air.

'Look and see if it's brought someone to visit us, Henny. I'm so limp from this heat.'

'Are you expecting somebody today?' Henny asked, getting up.

'You never know in the country.'

Henny walked up the earthen steps of a grassy hill to the left of the summerhouse; at the top of the hill was a gigantic weeping ash whose thick, leafy branches, bound into staves, were fastened around in a circle. With a round table encircled by benches in the centre, the ash looked like a giant open umbrella. On the side facing the fjord, a peephole had been made in the branches through which a person could look down at the steamship wharf.

'The Holms' housemaid, the Nissens' housekeeper, the Bertelsens' ironing board, a butcher's wife with dropsy, two gangly boys!' Henny called out, her face at the opening. 'A lady in a grey walking dress with a blue parasol. She must be coming here since she's going over to the gate.'

'Blond or dark?' asked Mrs. Reinertson, coming up to her sister.

'The knot at the back of her neck is blond. Now she's turning around, so the gate must be locked.'

'Let me see,' Mrs. Reinertson pushed Henny aside and peeked through the hole.

'Why, it's little Mrs. Gerner. What a pity that she'll have to tramp through the woods in this heat.'

'The Tivoli wife,' said Henny, wrinkling her nose. 'What do we want with her, Karen?'

'You know, I feel sorry for her. She has nobody, the poor thing. And with that dried up old stick of a husband.'

'Yes, I can't imagine being married to Theodor Gerner,' said Henny following Karen down the earthen steps. 'Such an obstinate, self-righteous man. And once when I was little, I saw him pick something disgusting out of his nose. I'll never forget it.'

'Now really, Henny,' said Mrs. Reinertson.

'Do you truly like her, Karen? Isn't it just because she's 'a woman with a past'?' Henny pronounced the last words in a mocking tone.

'Oh I don't know. I thought at first that I could help her a little. But she's so reserved I can't get through to her.'

'Wasn't she one of those – well, not to mince words – a woman of easy virtue?' Henny asked with a grimace.

'No Henny, it wasn't as bad as that! But even if she were – *we* marry what can only be called men of easy virtue.' Karen walked over to the corner of the house and looked down the footpath along the edge of the forest.

'Good day, Mrs. Gerner,' she called out soon after, walking a few quick steps downhill. 'This is very kind of you. Welcome!' She took both of Lucie's hands, in spite of the open parasol, and kissed her.

'This is my sister, Miss Brandt.' She led Lucie over to the summerhouse, where Henny had seated herself again. 'And this is Mrs. Gerner, Henny.'

Lucie greeted her and smiled but said nothing more.

'Do sit down.' Mrs. Reinertson pulled over a garden chair. 'We're sitting out here today because it's cooler. You can take a swim later on. Now you must rest a little.'

'Won't you take off your hat, Mrs. Gerner?' Henny asked, wanting to be friendly.

Lucie smiled, thanked her, and took off her hat.

'It's so beautiful here,' she said taking a deep breath. 'Living out here would almost have to make you a better person.'

'Yes, it is beautiful,' Mrs. Reinertson replied. 'And so secluded. With the fjord in front and the forest close up in back, you could really believe you're the only one here if you didn't know the country houses make a wreath around the island.

'But what are you reading that's so fascinating in that ragged old newspaper, Henny?' She turned toward her sister who was surreptitiously reading the sheet in which the shoes had been wrapped.

'It's about a women's rights meeting last winter. I just have two more lines.

'My goodness, this Mrs. Asmundsen is certainly getting raked over the coals.' Henny put the newspaper down. 'What did she actually say? I can hardly tell through all the insults.'

'Oh, she said that women can't talk about sexual morality because so many of them are sexless.'

'Is *that* anything to get so worked up about?' Henny asked.

'Yes, because now that this ruckus about morality has come up, they've changed their tune. It's not like before, when women were pleased to be regarded as angelic beings, so pure and spiritual in their love. Now, by Heaven, they're just as sensual as the men, and therefore men must kindly restrain themselves, just the way women have done.'

'But tell me,' Lucie said eagerly, 'do you think it's really true that women...' She stopped suddenly, encountering an attentive look from Henny, and blushed. 'Well I just thought – oh now I don't remember what I thought.'

'She must have said more than that,' Henny said, after a silence. 'The newspaper says that if her ideas spread, indecency will be legitimised.'

'Something to the effect that the situation now couldn't be worse, and it would never be any different until satisfying love's urges was no longer regarded as immorality.'

'And how is that going to happen?' Henny asked, putting her elbows on the table and resting her cheeks on her hands.

'Well at some point people will have to come to their senses and direct their work toward reforming life, instead of wasting their energy repressing their desires. And that's why all serious people should be social democrats.'

'Do you think that would help?'

'If society were run on social democratic principles, all this would resolve itself. Because the crux of the problem is economic. In politics we know that might makes right. In the domain of love it's the same, and here 'might' means the opportunity for both men and women to properly provide for themselves.'

'But are we just supposed to let morality follow the same old course?' Henny said heatedly. 'Because we can't all go off and become socialists!'

'Mrs. Asmundsen says that right now women have no more important duty than to arm and defend themselves. Every honest and reasonable person knows that the *Gauntlet*-demand is a pipe dream and it always will be. And so the only recourse, as far as possible, is to make sure they have the same past as the men. Then a woman wouldn't have to suffer agonies in marriage wondering about her husband's past. Nor would she be so devastated by his infidelity. She'd be better able to understand how things like that happened, and how to console herself. Marriages would be much happier in this regard.'

'I can't imagine how you remember so much of that,' Lucie said admiringly.

As Lucie gazed at her, she saw a shadow momentarily cross Mrs. Reinertson's face. She quickly turned her head. Pastor Brandt was standing in the doorway wearing a black topcoat, panama hat, white cravat, and the long gold lady's watch chain hanging outside his waistcoat.

'Oh there you are, Fredrik,' said Karen. 'You know Mrs. Gerner, of course.'

Lucie half rose in her chair and greeted him. Brandt bowed stiffly.

'Won't you sit here with us? Or what would you like to do?' Karen asked.

'If I'm not intruding,' he answered. He sat down on the bench next to Henny and gazed around absent-mindedly. 'You were having such a lively talk when I came in.' His voice was heavy and subdued.

'We were talking about the requirements for a happy marriage,' said Henny. 'Karen thinks that women should let themselves go.'

Karen made a face at Henny and looked at Brandt as if she felt sorry for him.

'When women in the highest levels of society sink to that level, it's a sign that the collapse of the state is near,' Brandt said quietly.

Karen bit her lip, and looked as if she was trying to restrain herself, but then she couldn't resist saying, 'That was true as long as women were angels. When angels sink or fall, then the end of the world must be near, but there's no imminent destruction when we're talking about human beings, as the example of men has demonstrated long enough. You don't use the word 'fall,' either, you say a man 'lives.''

'So you would calmly accept evil triumphing over good?' Brandt said mildly, with a sigh.

'Good is only what people say it is,' Karen answered. 'In the old days, it was considered good and appropriate to mutilate innocent women until they swore they were witches, then burn them afterwards. There is absolutely no crime in the world that hasn't been committed for the glory of God and the good of mankind.'

'Well, I'm not going to argue with you, Karen,' Brandt waved his hand. 'It's easy enough to refute you, but I'm not in the mood.'

'And isn't it the men who, in spite of the lives they've led, have produced everything we respect and honour?' Karen continued. 'And provided for us as well! They've kept their productive capacity undiminished. While women! – Well, they've been angels and women of pleasure – that's been their mission and their destiny. If we look at the results, there's nothing so horrifying about men's lives.'

'Indeed the women should really pipe down,' Brandt said with more animation. 'We're starting from fundamentally different premises, but I agree with your conclusion. And now all this fuss about women's rights. I ask you, don't they possess the greatest, the most tyrannical of all rights – handing out refusals to their victims? What more do they want?'

'As if men didn't refuse women, too,' Karen said.

'Oh the poor things! At least men don't start a flirtation with a woman, make her fancy they want to marry her, just to have the triumph of saying no afterwards. Oh no, women have little enough conscience to begin with, you shouldn't be so quick to give them even more rights.' Brandt got up.

'I'm so thirsty,' he said. 'No, don't get up.' He waved a hand at Henny and Karen, who both started to rise. 'I'll find what I want myself and I can ask Lina for seltzer water.'

> Oh, the misery of our life!
> Is there any joy on our earthly path
> That does not begin in glory
> And end in tears?
> There is no bliss that lasts forever!

He hummed as he slowly walked up the steps of the veranda.

'Tell me one thing,' said Henny after Brandt had left. 'What should be done with the children from these unsanctioned relationships?'

'Feed and clothe them according to one's ability, naturally,' answered Karen. 'If having children were no longer shameful, things would be simpler and different. And those who couldn't afford to have children wouldn't need to have any.'

'Did Mrs. Asmundsen say *that*?' cried Henny. 'Then I hardly wonder that they talk about criminal, pestilential doctrines. Really, Karen!'

'What a hypocritical, idiotic institution!' Mrs. Reinertson cried, waving at the paper on the table in front of Henny. 'As if men didn't practice it all the time, especially in the upper classes Fredrik talked about – as if it weren't recommended by doctors and the health police here in our virtuous, *Gauntlet*-festooned, hypocritical society.'

The housemaid came in and asked what kind of jam should be put on the table.

'I'm coming,' said Mrs. Reinertson, getting up. 'If you want to take a swim, there's just enough time before we eat,' she said to Lucie.

'I'll go and get the key,' said Henny running into the house.

Lucie was quite dazed. Never in her life had she felt so unsettled. So she was just as good as Theodor, and didn't need to be ashamed because she'd been like *that*. Oh God, knowledge and book learning and a mind like Mrs. Reinertson's! Oh what wonderful gifts they were. That was the reason she was so miserable and let Theodor browbeat her – because she didn't know anything and didn't think about anything. – The tears came in a rush. – Yes, and because Theodor knew nothing about the things Mrs. Reinertson had talked about either.

When Henny approached the summerhouse, the bathhouse key swinging by a ribbon on her finger, she saw that Lucie was weeping with a handkerchief pressed to her face. She came to an abrupt stop and walked back a short distance the way she had come. Then she began humming a snatch of song, and advanced again, walking as heavily as she could in her thin slippers.

'Here's the key, Mrs. Gerner.' She was half-turned toward the entrance, busily clearing some worm-eaten leaves from a rosebush and collecting them in the palm of her hand.

'Thank you,' Lucie said, clearing her throat to steady her voice.

'I'll walk down with you through the grounds,' Henny said, when Lucie reached for the key.

They walked by the lawn and the flowerbeds on the level area in front of the house, down the diagonal slope to the place where the gravel path divided into two routes down to the little gate in the rail fence. Directly below lay the steamship wharf, gleaming long and white in the sunshine.

'You feel like sitting down every place you look,' Lucie said, stopping by a mossy bench carved out of the rock face and overhung by creeping vines and a weeping birch.

'How about here?' replied Henny, who was further down the stone steps. 'In here under the spruce is the most delightful bench you can imagine. But we really have to hurry if we're going to be ready for dinner. I have to change my clothes, too.'

Outside the little gate, Henny handed the key to Lucie. 'You know the bathhouse. The third dock from the steamship wharf.'

XV
Evening

Later in the afternoon, after Brandt had left for town, Lucie sat with Mrs. Reinertson and Henny and had coffee under the weeping ash. Mrs. Reinertson read aloud a section of *The Commodore's Daughters**, with the promise to read more the following day. Afterwards they took a walk through the woods that encircled the island, and after supper, rowed out on the fjord among the wooded islets.

Mrs. Reinertson and Lucie took the oars, and Henny sat in the stern, singing so sweetly in the lovely evening that the people living nearby paused to listen.

Lucie was thinking about *The Commodore's Daughters*. She was struck again by the difference between proper ladies and someone like herself. In the book the brother was so careful that his sisters should not know or suspect the slightest thing about the relations between gentlemen and common girls.

Oh no, there was, and would always be, a whole sea of difference between the fine ladies and someone like herself. And there was no way to get across that sea. Take Theodor, for example. – He would have laughed in scorn if he had heard what Mrs. Reinertson said. And the things they wrote in the newspaper about Mrs. Asmundsen's lecture!

What would Theodor say when he found she had run off without his permission, without even leaving a message with Martine. She couldn't imagine how she'd had the nerve to do it. And then letting herself be talked into staying overnight. She had never intended to do anything but go home that evening. When he got the letter Mrs. Reinertson had persuaded her to write, saying she was staying a couple of days, oh Lord, oh Lord, he was going to be so furious. And as far as an answer was concerned – Mrs. Reinertson should never imagine that he would send one. It would be best for her to disappear right now and never show her face at home again.

She became so frightened that she actually felt cold in the soft warm summer air. Earlier in the day she'd thought it would serve him right to be upset, but now she was frightened and appalled by what she had done.

What if he was in such a rage that he demanded a divorce? Many times in the past when he was being mean and hateful she had thought that would be just fine, but now it seemed like the worst thing that could happen. Being the wife of a fine wealthy gentleman was nothing to sniff at, after all. Her life was comfortable and without care. That was something she should keep in mind. She had him to thank for everything, even for the fact that she was here with these fine and proper ladies, being treated as their equal. She should remember that, when he was being mean and hateful to her, more than she did.

No, not for anything in the world did she want to be divorced.

What was he going to do now, she wondered. Come out to get her, or send someone for her? Supposing the letter got lost and didn't reach him – he would probably report her disappearance to the police.

She was glad she had the oar to attend to, so she could be occupied every minute.

'These beautiful light nights,' said Mrs. Reinertson, when Henny stopped singing. 'It won't get any darker than it is now.'

'So beautiful,' Lucie said, tilting her head back to silence the sigh rising in her.

'And that star over there,' continued Mrs. Reinertson. 'It looks like a diamond. Norway is glorious in the summer.'

'Like a diamond,' Lucie repeated, wetting her dry lips with the tip of her tongue for the twentieth time.

Henny was now singing Grieg's melody to Vinje's poem 'My Dear Old Mother.'*

'Your eyes are so bright this evening,' said Mrs. Reinertson. 'Is it the song?'

Lucie nodded. The corners of her mouth quivered and a warm mist flooded her eyes. Oh how beautiful life could be, she thought, averting her head and taking slow, deliberate breaths.

'Good night Mrs. Gerner.' They had come up from the shore and were standing in the doorway that led from the backyard up to the bedrooms.

'Good night, Mrs. Reinertson. Thank you for the lovely day.'

'Now see that you sleep well and come down tomorrow, fresh and cheerful. If you sleep late, I'll send up a coffee tray and the letter from your husband.'

Lucie went upstairs. Her room faced the woods and its glass doors opened onto a little balcony.

'If only I hadn't done this,' she said to herself, walking restlessly back and forth. 'It's been lovely to be here, but I'll pay for it all right. A letter from Theodor! Not likely – we'd have to search high and low for that.'

She took off her dress and corset, then undid her braids. A wide bluish strip of light fell through the glass door and across the floor. The rest of the room was in twilight.

She walked back and forth a few times in the centre of the bright strip on the floor, then stopped by the door to the balcony and looked at the moon for a while. Hurrying back to the dressing table, she lit the lamps and stood there, gazing at her figure in the mirror.

'It's true, it *must* be true,' she muttered, sliding her fingers from her waist down over her hips. 'I've never had a stomach like this in my life. What if they knew, Mrs. Reinertson and Miss Brandt, that I'm afraid I'm having a baby by some jailbird or the like.

– 'And what about Theodor!

– 'Because there's no chance it's with *him*. No chance in the world.'

Oh nonsense. It wasn't absolutely certain, and even if… Maybe she'd have a miscarriage, like Mrs. Mørk did last winter. But that was because she kept doing her exercises too long.

What did they do in those exercise classes last winter?

She loosened her petticoats, let them slide down over her legs, and kicked them across the floor. With her hands on her hips, she stretched and twisted in every possible direction.

One, two, three, four, she raised herself up on tiptoe and, heels together, bent her knees until she was sitting on her haunches, then she straightened up again. 'One, two, three, four.'

She kept it up until she lost her balance and tumbled over on the floor.

Then she sat for a bit, caught her breath, got up and started a new exercise, which she then followed by others.

Finally she went over and propped the balcony door open, stepped up on a chair and hung by her arms from the doorjamb.

'I can't do any more.' She released her grip and let herself fall.

Instantly she was up again. Then down. Then up, until finally, gasping from the exertion, she undressed completely and put on the night-gown.

'It's so long! Imagine, Mrs. Reinertson is that much taller than me.'

She turned her head and shoulders to look down at the back of her night-gown. 'It's like having a train.'

She took hold of the front and lifted it slightly so she wouldn't step on it as she walked over and blew out the lamp.

'I'm so wonderfully tired,' she murmured, lying down in bed and luxuriously stretching her limbs.

'I'm tingling all over.'

XVI
Lucie

'You'll see, Gerner will come in person this evening since he hasn't written,' Mrs. Reinertson said the next afternoon as they were walking in the forest.

'Lord knows,' Lucie answered, with an anxious sigh. 'It would probably be best if I went home.'

'Absolutely not. Wait and see. It's doing you good to be here. If you don't get a letter tonight, you can leave tomorrow morning.'

'I'm afraid he'll be angry that I've stayed so long. I was just going to stay for a short visit.'

'Silence means approval,' Mrs. Reinertson said. 'If he were angry, he would certainly write.'

She doesn't know Theodor very well, if she thinks silence means approval, Lucie thought. When he's silent he's the most furious, and I have no idea what he'll do to me after this – I don't even dare think about it. I might as well stay until tomorrow because he'll make the same uproar whether I come today or tomorrow. At least I can have some peace in the meantime.

When they got back to the house, they found Lieutenant Reinertson sitting on the bottom step of the veranda stairs. He was leaning forward with his arms on his knees and a cigar in his mouth. At the sight of the women, he sprang to his feet and greeted them.

'Why didn't you come in time for dinner, Knut?' asked Mrs. Reinertson. 'That's what we do in the country.'

'I was hoping to make an impression with my modest behaviour, Aunt,' Knut answered, looking at his cap, which he was twirling around on his index finger.

'You're still using the same old tricks to ingratiate yourself?' asked Henny.

'Yes of course, because I've not forgotten that they always made you laugh,' Knut said with a mischievous smile.

'But Lord, it gets so tiresome after a while,' Henny said, tossing her head. 'It was all right once upon a time, but you – you'll never grow up.'

'What can you expect after such a neglected upbringing.' Knut kept his eyes on his cap, which continued to spin. 'For two years now I've had to do without your precious admonitions, and in all that time old Adam has gone unchecked.'

Lucie gazed at Knut with shining eyes, laughing out loud at everything he said. What a charming man he was!

'I suppose you think that you're terribly amusing,' said Henny, walking past Knut up the veranda steps. 'But I don't think so.'

'Are you two at it again?' Mrs. Reinertson said, sitting down on a garden chair. 'Declare peace now, once and for all.'

'It's only because she's in love with me!' Knut cried, tossing his cap in the air.

'You are a fool, Knut Reinertson,' said Henny indifferently from the top step, turning her head toward him. 'A stupid, conceited fool.'

'No, not foolish, but conceited!' he quickly retorted, taking little steps with his arm outstretched to catch his cap on his index finger as it fell. 'A little bit conceited, but not foolish, isn't that right, Aunt Reinertson? Henny could do worse than fall in love with me, don't you think?' He popped his cap on his head and looked boldly at Mrs. Reinertson.

Henny remained in the same position, her head turned back toward the garden, attempting to look severe, but she couldn't manage it. Reluctantly her mouth widened into a smile and a little dimple in her left cheek appeared.

'Oh yes, how about that slovenly little orderly of yours,' Mrs. Reinertson said. 'He was worse than you.'

'Well, what do you say, Mrs. Gerner?' Knut said to Lucie. 'I'm not so bad, am I?'

Lucie laughed heartily, and didn't answer.

'You mustn't be such an appreciative audience, Mrs. Gerner!' Henny cried. 'Otherwise he'll bore us to death with his banal remarks. – Tivoli laughter,' she muttered with a scowl, as she walked into the house.

'Won't you sit down, Mrs. Gerner, or perhaps you'd like to go in?' Mrs. Reinertson rose and went up the veranda steps.

'Come for a walk around the grounds instead,' Knut said, setting off along the lawn.

Lucie followed him, flushed with pleasure.

'It's a charming place,' Knut said when they had reached the lowest terrace. 'And so well maintained!'

'Yes, it's really delightful here. I should say so.' Lucie hopped down and seated herself on a bench, with her back leaning against the mossy stone wall of the terrace.

Knut stretched out on his stomach on the terrace above. His chin was resting on his crossed arms and his face was so close to the back of Lucie's head that she could feel his breath on her ear and cheek.

'And what a view,' Lucie said, pointing to the fjord.

'From here it's much more beautiful,' Knut said, looking at Lucie's white neck with its little golden tendrils.

'Do you see something I don't?'

'Your neck. And you know what? I simply can't resist.' He kissed her neck beneath her ear.

'Are you crazy, Lieutenant, what if somebody saw that? And I'll have you know I'm not that kind of woman.'

'Oh yes you are,' Knut said, calmly taking her by the shoulders and pressing his face into her soft throat.

Oh Lord, Lucy thought, he's doing it anyway – and me, a married woman and everything. And here at Mrs. Reinertson's. It's just because it's me. She wanted to get up and run away from him, but a shiver of pleasure ran through her body and she was powerless. Memories of gay and lustful hours from the old days overcame her, and with closed eyes, she leaned her head back and let him kiss her mouth.

'Come down here on the bench with me,' she whispered.

Knut let go of her shoulders and stood up. 'We have to go back up,' he said. 'They'll be expecting us for tea.'

He's being careful, thought Lucie, as they were on their way back. Lord, he's so sweet! I could eat him right up! And now I know he's in love with me.

'Do you remember last winter when we were dancing together, Lieutenant Reinertson?' she asked.

'When I was a monk, yes!' He was walking ahead of Lucie and answered without pausing or turning around.

'I had such fun that night,' said Lucie. 'I'll never forget it.'

'Come and have tea!' Henny's voice came from the veranda steps. 'Where are you?'

'It's a good thing we didn't stay any longer,' Lucie whispered in his ear.

He shrugged slightly without looking at her.

An hour later Mrs. Reinertson and Lucie were sitting on the veranda steps, speaking softly whenever they had something to say, so they wouldn't disturb Knut, who was attempting to hypnotise Henny in the summerhouse, where a lamp was burning.

When they heard Henny laugh merrily, they hurried in.

'It didn't work?'

'No, it's no use with Henny,' Knut said dejectedly. 'It proves she was brought into the world to vex and defame me.'

'He thought I was asleep and started giving me orders – the simpleton!' Henny burst out laughing again.

'Let me try with you then, Aunt,' Knut begged.

'No, not tonight, my dear. Try it with Mrs. Gerner, if she's willing.'

Lucie was willing.

'Well, you go out then. I need silence, first and foremost.'

Mrs. Reinertson and Henny sat down outside and Lucie was seated on a chair. Knut stood behind her next to the lamp, which illuminated a watch he had placed in her hand and told her to stare at it.

After three minutes had gone by, he walked quietly around to face her and repeatedly ran his fingertips from her temples down along her arms. Then he took the watch out of her hand. Her arm and hand remained in the same position.

'Now you can't straighten your arm,' he said softly. 'Try it.'

The muscles in Lucie's face contracted slightly and then came a faint, strained, 'No.'

'Next Friday at exactly seven o'clock in the evening you will come to see me,' Knut whispered the order. 'I live on Ullevålsveien, number 34, on the second floor. Do you understand?'

The lips parted slowly in Lucie's utterly lifeless face, and with difficulty she said, 'yes.'

'Seven o'clock next Friday, the 27th of July,' he repeated softly, but distinctly.

Then he walked out and beckoned.

'Oh really, that's horrible,' Mrs. Reinertson burst out, when she saw Lucie's stiff face and bent, upraised arm.

'Stand up,' ordered Knut.

Slowly and heavily, Lucie stood up.

'Your name is Hans, isn't that right?'

'Yes,' she said with great effort.

'And your husband is dead, isn't that right?'

'Yes.'

'Come here and feel this,' he whispered to Henny.

Mrs. Reinertson walked over and tried to straighten Lucie's arm. 'It's as hard as stone,' she said with a shudder.

'Of course you can straighten your arm,' Knut said encouragingly. 'Stretch it out.'

Instantly Lucie stretched out her arm.

'Go over and sit down on the bench, but lift your skirt, you see how muddy it is.'

With her left hand, Lucie took hold of her skirt and lifted it above her ankles. Then she leaned forward slightly and began walking with tentative steps.

'But it's quite dry here, you see. Let go of your skirt and stand still.'

Instantly she did what he said.

'Stop now, Knut,' said Mrs. Reinertson. 'This is too horrible to watch.'

'Right away, Aunt,' Knut said, walking over close to Lucie.

'Five minutes after you wake up you'll go in and get a glass of water for Aunt Reinertson. Five minutes after you wake up. Do you hear?'

'Yes,' Lucie said in the same somnambulant tone as before.

'Wake up!' he breathed on her.

She immediately opened her eyes and gazed around her with a blank, wondering look and a timid air. Then she carefully sat down on the bench and started to rub her knees and move her upper body back and forth.

'Now you're what I call a medium, Mrs. Gerner!' Knut said, and then they all talked at once about what she had done.

Lucie looked from one to the other as if she didn't understand.

'Do you really not know anything about it?' Henny asked looking at her curiously.

'I remember getting so heavy and sleepy,' Lucie answered, rubbing her eyes.

'You're not feeling ill after all that?' Mrs. Reinertson asked sympathetically.

'No, just a little tender in my head and knees.'

They sat in silence, glancing over at Lucie, who was still rubbing her knees. Then she suddenly became restless, stood up and walked to the door, came back and sat down, pressing her hands to her head as if she were pondering something. This was repeated several times. Then she quickly walked out.

'You see, exactly five minutes have gone by,' Knut said, pointing at his watch, which was still lying on the table.

'Really, this is absolutely criminal,' Mrs. Reinertson said, shifting abruptly in her seat.

Immediately afterward, Lucie came back with a water glass on a tray, which she set in front of Mrs. Reinertson.

Knut's eyes widened in amazement as he looked at Lucie.

'This is terrible!' Henny cried, running out of the summerhouse. 'I'll be blessed if I stay under the same roof with a sorcerer.'

'But out here under the open sky you can't possibly have any objections,' said Knut, who had run after her and boldly put his arm through Henny's. 'Let's walk around a bit in the moonlight and smell the flowers.' He inhaled deeply. 'It makes one feel so delightfully melancholy.'

'Oh – melancholy?'

'Yes, because one falls into thoughts about improving oneself – which amounts to the same thing.'

'Take care that you don't miss the steamboat,' said Henny, when they had walked for a while without speaking.

'Are you eager to get rid of me, Henny?'

'I'm just trying to be helpful, you know.'

'Well thank you, but I'd rather you wouldn't. Actually, I've arranged to have a boat come for me, so I can stay as long as I like.'

'As long as we'll let you, I suppose you mean.'

'I mean, I'd like to have a talk with you.'

'Henny, come help me! And you, too, Knut!' Mrs. Reinertson's frightened voice reached them.

'What's wrong with her?' Alarmed, Henny bent over Lucie, who was lying full length on the summerhouse floor, white and unmoving.

'Unfasten her dress, Henny.' Mrs. Reinertson dipped her handkerchief in water and placed it on Lucie's forehead. 'All of a sudden she jumped up off the bench, turned dead white, and fell down there. This is what comes of your hypnosis, Knut.'

'Come help us!' said Henny, kneeling beside Lucie and tearing open the buttons of her dress. 'Just like a man to stand there gaping!'

Knut bent over Lucie, blew on her face and called: 'Wake up!'

'Oh that's a big help,' said Mrs. Reinertson. 'Crouch down behind her and support her back. That's the way. Thank God, she's opening her eyes. Let's get her up on her feet.'

'You'd better go up and lie down,' Mrs. Reinertson said, when Lucie was restored to consciousness again. 'Take my arm and I'll walk with you.'

'Shall I help you, Aunt?' asked Knut.

'No thank you, it's really not necessary.'

XVII
Henny

'Come, let's sit up on the veranda, Henny!' Knut took her hand and drew her along with him. 'There, now.' He had pressed her down onto a side bench under the thick vines that covered the veranda's walls and ceiling. 'Now I have to say to myself: May God grant you strength, Knut.'

'Oh, shouldn't we go back down to the summerhouse,' Henny said. 'It's a bit dark here, I think.'

'Oh no! I'd never be able to say it if I knew you could see me. I came out here to propose to you Henny. There, now it's said, thank God.' He exhaled in relief. 'And now you can do whatever you want with me.'

Henny was silent and unmoving.

'Don't you have anything to say?' he asked, after waiting a little while.

'You said you wanted to propose to me. Go ahead, I'm all ears.'

'Don't make fun of me. I *have* proposed to you. Do you want me to get down on my knees and beg for your hand and heart?'

'Are you seriously proposing to be my husband?'

'Yes, I certainly am! I know very well that I'm far from worthy of you, but it must be my love that gives me courage. I've loved you for five years and 10½ months.'

'So you've counted the days?' Henny could hardly keep from smiling. She could clearly see the contours of his bare curly head, his broad shoulders and the buttons of his uniform glittering in the moonlight. He was hunched forward with his face turned toward hers. His arm lay across his knee and his hand hung down, gleaming white.

'It started that time at Uncle Reinertson's summer ball, here on this veranda, right where we're sitting, as a matter of fact. You came over and asked me to help you with your glove, do you remember that?'

'No, I don't remember. Ugh, these mosquitoes,' she waved away the buzzing insects. 'You were a mere boy at the time.'

'I was 20 years old, and a cadet as well.'

'But I was 22 and only interested in older men.'

'Yes, thank you, I noticed that, and you can be sure I said a blessing over my youth.' He straightened up, and broke off a branch that was brushing against his face. 'What a delightful ball that was. I was like a wounded bird, running out in the garden to hide because I didn't want to dance, then running back to see who you were dancing with.' He sat in silence for a while, pulling the leaves off the broken branch, one by one. 'It was really irresponsible, what you did,' he blurted out. 'Why did you ask me to button that stupid glove?'

'You were just standing there, I suppose. What was so wrong with that?'

'Well if *you* hadn't done *that*, it would never have crossed my mind.' He snapped the broken branch into little pieces and tossed them away.

'How many times had I been with you, year after year, and not seen anything special about you. I heard people say you were beautiful, of course, but I wasn't even sure that was true. But then up you walk, with your innocent, trusting face and stick your beautiful wrist in my face. Merciful God, something came over me! I started to shake, had hot and cold flashes – and the way you smiled when you thanked me. A man would have had to be superhuman to resist it. Are you laughing at me?'

'Yes, because it sounds so comic. Oh look at the moon, it's all the way out now.'

'It's been anything but comic for me. I've been walking around like a person who's half sick. It's a wonder I've got as far as I have.'

'Oh I can imagine you've been hard at work – the way you've been *carousing* from ball to ball.' Henny crossed her arms tightly over her breast and leaned back on the bench, so that her head was almost hidden by the hanging branches.

'I suppose you'd rather have had me go off and become a drunkard? You never gave me a chance to propose to you, although I often thought you were fond of me too.'

'Yes, fond of you – but I really couldn't become engaged to a fellow who's so giddy, and younger than I am to boot.'

'My God, those poor, harmless two years! You'd see how steady and reliable I would be if you said yes.'

'Oh God knows – you're much too immature. I'd be ashamed of myself!'

'Oh, I don't think *that* would be necessary. Try me, give me a two-month trial and see if I haven't changed. Can you blame a man who is so sick and tired of everything that he needs to look for something amusing from time to time, so he doesn't go off and hang himself? Think how faithful I've been, Henny. For these two years you've been away, I've longed for you constantly and grown surer and surer that I will never love anybody else. I think it's quite touching, I really do.'

'Oh I believe you've loved many women. Or at least you've flirted with them by the dozens. You have a reputation for being fresh and pushy, and, not to mince words, a scoundrel where women are concerned.'

'Yes, that's very possibly true,' he said meekly. 'I've certainly not always behaved the way you would like, but it all comes back to the same cause. Besides, I've only flirted to the extent they allowed me. You never get any further than that.'

'Not with ladies, no, but what about the others?'

'Do I have to confess *that* too?'

'Yes, it's better if I know the truth.'

He paused for a moment. 'I've gone to them, like other men do' – he cleared his throat – 'less often than most, as far as that goes.'

'Well, why are you stopping?'

'Surely I'm not supposed – to go into details, am I? There *isn't* anything more. I've never seduced a housemaid.'

Henny sat in silence.

'So you want a *Gauntlet*-man, is that it? Then you'll have to meet somebody who's just been released from Gaustad.'

'No, I don't want anything to do with *Gauntlet*-men. I have that much sense at least.'

'Then why won't you accept me, Henny? Think of being two people in the world instead of one. We would be so happy together – like two yolks in an egg. – And you have so much money, too, Henny.'

'So you've thought about that as well.'

'Of course, otherwise I would never have dared to offer myself, Henny – even if I were dying of love for you. Me, with my lieutenant's wages and my tutoring.'

'You are an amazingly strange fellow, you truly are. But it's impossible to be angry with you.'

'Is *that* wrong, too? That I don't pretend I'm in despair because you're rich? Money is essential if you're going to have any fun, and does it matter which one of us has it? So give in and say yes, Henny. I promise you won't regret it.'

'Now you listen to me,' Henny said, after some thought. 'You've explained yourself and your past, and you think that nothing about it should be an impediment. Now it's my turn. I have my own confession to make, because I'm a woman with a past.'

He flinched. 'You! I don't understand what you mean by that,' he stammered, fumbling for words. 'Oh you're just joking,' he said with a sudden jerk toward her.

'No, I'm not joking. What I said is true, and now we'll see if you're willing to believe me when I assure you that it doesn't mean the slightest thing, and that you should marry me regardless.'

'Then you'll have me?' he burst out jubilantly, leaping to his feet. Then he sank down onto the bench and sat as if turned to stone.

'Now it's my turn to ask if you will have me.'

He didn't answer, just sat staring down at his knees and his hands resting on them. In the moonlight that now flooded into the room, they seemed even whiter than in the daylight.

'Past,' he said finally, without moving. 'What kind of past?'

'I had some lovers when I was in Paris.'

'Some,' he turned from side to side. 'As many as that?'

'Yes, now you know. You see, I'm just as honest as you.'

'Well thank you, I can't claim that I'm exactly pleased about that.' He was speaking so quietly that Henny could scarcely hear what he said. 'Lovers – that you – you know – lived with?'

'Yes, that I lived with.'

'Frenchmen?'

'Yes, no – well, one was French.'

'And the others…'

'Oh what difference does it make.'

'Difference!' He leaped up, wildly waving his arms. 'I could strangle – murder – stomp the life out of them!' he spoke through clenched teeth. 'Tear them limb from limb and throw the pieces in the sea – blood, blood – Oh the thought of it – those monsters robbing you of your pure innocence, Henny.' His voice trailed off, trembling and almost cracking with sorrow. He slid back down on the bench into his previous posture.

His violent outburst had frightened Henny. She had got to her feet and reached out her arm as if to quiet him. Now she sat down again and said, 'This way the match is more equal. Birds of a feather…'

Knut barely moved for some time. Henny looked at him out of the corner of her eye. She saw his head suddenly sink to his chest and then heard him quietly weeping.

She rose and stood in front of him.

'You haven't answered my question. Do you want me regardless?' she asked placing her hand on his shoulder.

'Do I want you, Henny?' he said, looking up at her with brimming eyes and tear-streaked cheeks. 'What a question – but it hurts, it hurts so much.' His voice choked and he had to pause a while to master it. 'If you had a reputation as the worst woman in the city, I would still kneel down and beg you to take me as your husband.' His head was tilted back and the moonlight was falling across his face as he looked up at Henny helplessly. 'I know very well that you have never believed in my love – do you believe in it now?'

Henny was greatly moved. Her breast rose and fell as she gasped for air, struggling to force out the words. But she could not. So she gave up, put her arms around Knut's neck, then sank down on his chest and pressed her face against his throat.

'Yes, Knut, now I believe in your love. And I love you, too. I believe in you, and I'm yours. Since you will have me.'

'Thank you, my beloved,' he whispered.

'And now I have something to tell you, Knut.' – Henny had got control of her emotions and was sitting on the bench beside Knut, with her hand in his. 'It's all a pack of lies.'

'What is a pack of lies?'

'That business about lovers, of course, you dunce! It's just proof of how young you are. I was only putting you to the test. You've passed it like a man. I'm proud of you, Knut.'

'Is that true, Henny?' he said hoarsely, pressing her hand against his heart.

'Of course it's true – unfortunately, I might almost say. Karen claims that for a marriage to be happy, *she* also has to have a past.'

Without a word, Knut slid down off the bench onto his knees, hid his face in Henny's lap, and cried like a child.

Henny tenderly stroked her fingers through his soft, thick hair and quieted him. 'My own boy, my sweet, kind Knut, my dear, only beloved – you should be happy.'

'That was happiness,' Knut said in a faint voice as he was getting to his feet. 'You shouldn't have done it, Henny. What if I'd had a heart attack?' He hurriedly wiped his face with a handkerchief.

'Karen will wonder where I've gone,' Henny said. 'Come on, let's go and get the lamp.' She ran down the veranda steps, followed by Knut.

When Henny entered the summerhouse, she sat down on the bench and rubbed her hands together enthusiastically. 'So now I'm engaged – how amusing that is! And it's none too soon either. But my goodness, how surprised Karen will be.'

'Yes,' said Knut. 'I'm sure she doesn't believe you would accept me.'

'Quite reasonably! But just look at you, Knut! Red splotches on your cheeks, and what's the matter with your eyes? Look here,' she ran over to him and gave his shoulders a little shake. – 'Why haven't you kissed me? On the mouth, I mean.' – She puckered her lips and raised them up to him.

He pulled his head back and took her by the wrists. 'I won't do that tonight, Henny, because I kissed someone else earlier today.'

'Really, Knut! You are *too* disgusting!' Henny knitted her brows and pulled her hands free. 'Who have you kissed?'

'Her, Mrs. Gerner.'

'The Tivoli wife. Here in our house! This evening? Then you're having an affair with her.'

'Certainly not. I've just been in her company once before and I haven't thought about her for a second since.'

'Then it's a thousand times worse. Is that the kind of person you are? Aren't you ashamed?'

'Yes, a little.'

'Kissed the Tivoli wife! When? How did you manage that little escapade, you disgusting thing?'

'When we were walking around the grounds.'

'So you immediately seized your chance. Yes, that's you all over. And at the exact time you were planning to propose to me.'

'You were being so scornful toward me. Nothing will come of it tonight either, I thought, so I did it in anger.'

'But what about her? Is she still the kind of woman who lets herself be kissed?'

'Well who doesn't? And especially her!'

'That tart. Karen should know about it. And as for you. What a delightful husband I'm getting.'

Henny clasped her hands behind her back and leaned her shoulder against the summerhouse wall by the door. She glared at Knut.

'If I can live with you day in and day out, Henny, it will be just as impossible for me to do something like that as it is for you, Henny. I will never betray you – you can see that already.'

'You just try it.'

Knut came closer and gripped Henny's arms above the elbows. 'You should be kind and gentle to me, Henny, I need that so much.' He put his head on her shoulder and closed his eyes. 'I know I'll be faithful to you, but what's the good of making promises. When you've been married to me for five years, see if you don't know it yourself.'

Henny turned her face and kissed his forehead.

'I've still got one thing to confess to you,' Knut said, taking Henny in his arms. 'After I'd hypnotised her, Mrs. Gerner – I gave an order – to visit me – in my room next week.'

Henny recoiled; she wanted to tear herself loose, but Knut held her and embraced her more tightly.

'Now you know me, in all my irresponsible nakedness, Henny. You mustn't push me away from you. I could have kept quiet about it. But I couldn't, and you can see it's a sign that I'm becoming a new person. I've *already* become one. Why I did it, I don't know, I've never wanted her at all, not before either, when I didn't have you – it was a momentary impulse, a boy's prank. That's the way I've behaved, but deep down I'm good all the same.'

When they parted, Henny pressed her lips against his mouth. It was a little while before they could tear themselves away from each other.

Henny tiptoed up the steps and slipped off her shoes in the hall so she wouldn't wake up her sister. But when she came in and was getting undressed, Karen suddenly said from the bed, 'I think Mrs. Gerner is going to have a baby. That must be why she's so nervous.'

Henny went over and sat down on the edge of the bed.

'I'm so happy, Karen.'

'Oh, why is that?' asked Karen, surprised by her tone and expression.

'I'm engaged to marry Knut, and I'm so happy, Karen, so happy, so happy.'

'Sit still, Henny. You're jiggling the bed.'

'Aren't you going to wish me joy, Karen?'

'Just last night you were saying you would never get married, Henny.'

'Yes, imagine! It wasn't until tonight that I realised I've always loved Knut.'

'That's nonsense, Henny! But it's fine as far as I'm concerned. Fancy, Knut, that boy!'

'He's a man, Karen.'

'Yes, of course, let's not argue about that. Well, well, my dear

Henny, God grant that it goes well for you. Knut is decent enough, I've always liked him, I have, but husbands are rubbish.'

'I believe in love, in spite of everything,' Henny said, lying down with her sister and putting her arms around her neck. 'I *can't* help it. And I believe in Knut. We *have* to believe in love, Karen – it *is* and always will be the most important thing in the world.'

'Yes, of course, yes. So you will be Mrs. Reinertson, too, the same as me. I hope you'll be very happy, Henny. It's so painful not to be.'

XVIII
Gerner

Gerner had passed through a succession of moods in the last few days. At first he had been concerned for her. To be sure, it wasn't unusual for Lucie to just walk out of the house when they'd had a scene, but before she had always come back in an hour or two. In time for meals, in any case.

What if she had gone out and done away with herself. People *could* take their own lives, that was a fact. Or what if she'd run away, out of the city, back to Kragerø. She was still something of a free spirit after all.

When he returned from the office late in the afternoon and found her letter, he read it with mounting fury. Never had he felt such bitterness toward her. So she was at Mrs. Reinertson's house in the country, happy and at ease, while he had been terrified, chastising himself, yes, actually remorseful. And there might be men out there playing up to her. Yes, of course there were. Mrs. Reinertson always had lots of company, especially now that Henny was there. He was actually looking forward to telling her off when she came home that evening, for the thought never crossed his mind that she would dare stay when she didn't hear from him. He would have had time to write, so she could have received his letter by the nine o'clock boat; when it didn't come, of course she would take the ten o'clock boat and be home at ll:00.

When the hours passed and she had not appeared by midnight, his feelings changed again. He felt humiliated and strangely impoverished. He was gripped by a nagging premonition that he had squandered her love and his power over her. And he longed to see her.

It was so empty and comfortless in the house.

Restlessly he paced the rooms. Everything that reminded him of her was like a stab wound. This was how it would be if she were dead, he thought, and then was overwhelmed by how much he would grieve, in spite of everything. His feelings softened, grew tender and mild, like those of a young boy. He had wronged Lucie terribly, but from now on, things would be better. He promised himself that.

If only she would come. Not a murmur of displeasure would she hear. He would pat her cheek and say: 'Well, Lucie, did you enjoy yourself out there, my dear?'

But he understood perfectly well what had happened. She had waited for his letter, naturally, until the last boat came. Then Mrs. Reinertson had persuaded her to stay the night – it was nice that people were so fond of Lucie. – When no letter arrived in the morning either, she would hurry to town as soon as she was dressed. Perhaps she'd arrive before he left for the office. In any case, she'd be there when he came home at midday for dinner. He would just be sweet and gentle with her.

When the entire next day passed and she hadn't appeared, his mood towards her grew bitter again. To pass the time, he walked down to Tivoli, where he met a business acquaintance with whom he had a few toddies. He got home late and fell into a dull rage when he realised she had still not come. The next morning he woke up late with a headache after the unaccustomed drinking, and had trouble doing his work at the office.

He went home for dinner a little earlier than usual, telling himself that of course she wouldn't be there, but he became genuinely alarmed when he found he was right.

None of this made sense. So shameless and defiant, so outrageously insulting – even *she* wouldn't treat him this way. She must have fallen sick. That could possibly explain it. But no, then Mrs. Reinertson would have written.

She wasn't out there any more – of course! It was impossible – she couldn't be there, perfectly at ease as if nothing was the matter, while he was in such agony. She must have taken off for town and not dared come home again. God only knew where she was now.

No, there would be no after-dinner nap today either. He got up from the chaise longue, where he had just settled himself. He felt too restless to nap. Poor Lucie, what might she have done in her distress? She had to be at least as miserable as he was. It was annoying that he absolutely had to go back to the office this afternoon, but this evening, as soon as he could manage, he would take the boat out to Malmø and ask when she had left there.

The whole time he was at the office, whether speaking to someone or writing, he thought only of Lucie. Surely she would never have turned to Nilsen? Oh no, she knew very well that would be the worst thing she could do to him. But what if she did. – Should he go to Nilsen and ask about her? Ugh, no – that vulgar creature – he couldn't bring himself to that. He hadn't seen her since the time he actually had to usher her out of his office. What a scene that was. He leaned back with his neck on the edge of the chair, and stared up at the ceiling. Here he had wanted to help her, so she would leave Lucie alone. – And then she got it into her head that he was after her – when the very thought of her sickened him. The woman was half crazy, of course. He stood up, took a few steps and sat down again. Send a messenger to Nilsen and ask. – But she was married to some fellow now and had probably moved. – Although he could surely track her down.

But first he would go home and see.

What if Lucie's coat was hanging in the hallway! His heart was pounding as he walked up Karl-Johan. He wouldn't flare up, but would speak to her calmly and sensibly. The poor thing – of course this had been at least as miserable for her as for him.

XIX
Homecoming

In the meantime, home at Incognitogaten, Lucie was pacing restlessly. She had decided to come back on the four o'clock boat, when Theodor was at the office, so she could avoid meeting him right away.

She wondered how she should act when he arrived. She couldn't decide if she should be contrite or cocky, beg forgiveness or behave as if nothing had happened.

'It doesn't make any difference how I act,' she said to herself, he'll be just as nasty either way.' She felt as if she could see and hear him, with his scornful face, those icy eyelids, and that voice!

'Oh Lord, Lord! If only I'd stayed out there!' She stood by Gerner's writing desk, fiddling with the newspapers and papers that lay there, picking up small objects and abruptly dropping them.

'This won't end well. Never in the world will this end well.

'Why am I staring at his stupid seal?' She put down his large silver-mounted seal with the lion head on its handle, which she had been regarding intently for some time.

'Ugh, my shoes are squeaky. Look at that chair.' She pushed her foot against a chair that was in her way, then moved it back again.

'So much dust in the air. And look how it sticks – I can't rub it off with my hand anyway.

'This won't end well, won't end well.

'The way that darling fellow kissed me!' She clapped her hands and darted into the sitting room where she paced back and forth, back and forth. 'The way he kissed me, ha, ha, just what Theodor deserves. Lord, what a fit he'd have if he knew.

'There, I felt it move again.' She stopped suddenly and put her hand to her heart. 'Now there's no doubt about it any more.

'God, I was so frightened last night the moment I felt it was alive. I wonder if I screamed or said something? Oh no, I'm sure I didn't do that.

'And then waking up in the Lieutenant's arms. Oh, so wonderful being held with those gentle white hands. So stupid of me not to pretend to faint again, so he'd have to hold me longer. I could see very well how irritated he was because he couldn't come up with me. He gave me such a melting look.

'I expect he'll come for a visit some day soon. If only Theodor isn't home.

'Look how ugly I am – yellow blotchy cheeks and such dull eyes. Yes, you do look lovely – just deserts for your acts.' She stuck out her tongue at her reflection in the mirror.

'Theodor will be able to tell when he looks at me, now that it's showing like this. Even since last night it's gotten much worse. Probably because I'm sure now.

'Well, no doubt he'll be happy. It's just what he's always wanted, and what do I care whose child it is. It's his own fault. – Being so horrid out in the street in the middle of the night. What can you do with someone like that. Serves him right.

'Oh my Lord! My Lord, there he is! There he is! – Into the bedroom – hide behind the sofa – No, no, too late. Sit here, this nice big chair, the back toward Theodor's door. – That's good, blinds down. – He won't see me right away.'

As soon as Gerner opened the front door, he saw Lucie's hat and parasol and the little grey jacket that matched her dress. As if by a puff of wind, his gentle mood blew away.

'Well, it's about time.'

He entered his own room first, busied himself with something at his desk, strolled back and forth a few times, and cleared his throat loudly. Then he made a tack toward the doorway and peered around the curtain into the sitting room.

'Where in the world is she?'

He walked through the dining room and bedroom, into the

kitchen, all of which were empty, then hurried across the kitchen and knocked on the maid's door.

'No of course not. God knows why we keep a maid,' he snarled, striding with long steps out into the hall to reassure himself that Lucie's clothes were really hanging there.

'Have you been sitting here the whole time?' He had entered the sitting room through the hall door and was standing right in front of Lucie.

'Yes.'

'And you heard me walking around looking for you?'

She didn't answer.

'And you've finally condescended to come home again?'

Lucie mumbled something inaudible.

'Where have you been?'

'You know very well.' She looked at him defiantly. 'I wrote to you.'

Gerner thrust his hands in his pants' pockets and looked at Lucie, his face rigid.

'Have you been on Malmø the whole time?' he asked. He pronounced each word slowly and deliberately.

'Where else would I have been?'

He turned on his heel, strode into his room, and paced the floor for most of an hour.

'If you please, tea is served,' Martine announced.

'I'd better not let him think I'm afraid of him,' thought Lucie, who still hadn't moved from the chair.

'Shall we have some tea?' Lucie walked past Gerner into the dining room, where Martine had lit the hanging lamp and rolled down the blinds.

Gerner was so angry that he was having trouble controlling himself. He had thought about leaving without granting her another word. But then he said to himself, 'Of course that's what she wants,' and decided to stay home. When he came into the dining room, Lucie was standing there pouring tea. As he was sitting down at the table, he caught a glimpse of her figure from the side, and he started.

'She's pregnant.'

He was so certain of his judgement that he didn't have to look at her again.

'It's true, even if she doesn't know it herself.'

A feeling of joy rose in him.

'The poor thing, that's why she's been so cross recently. If I'd had any idea, I would have been more considerate. How could she possibly not know it?'

Lucie was stirring her tea with downcast eyes and a somewhat wry expression.

'Don't you want to eat?' Gerner asked. His voice was so gentle that Lucie was surprised.

'I have a toothache,' she answered, feeling her side teeth with the tip of her tongue.

'That's not so unusual,' he said almost timidly.

'Oh, and why not?' she gave him a quick, suspicious look.

'That often goes along with it. Because in case you don't know, I can tell you that you're expecting.'

She turned fiery red. 'That's nonsense!' she almost screamed. She felt an irresistible urge to deny it.

'Well, tomorrow we can send for Mørk.'

Should I let Mørk come and pretend I don't know? Lucie thought. No, just let him believe I didn't want to say anything.

'Leave Mørk out of it,' she said curtly. 'Yes, of course I'm expecting, since you must know.'

Confirmation from her own mouth softened his mood even more.

'If only you had told me, Lucie. Then I would have been able to understand much better the things about you that have frightened me. I would have been more patient with you if I had known.'

His kindness irritated her. Now that he was expecting a child by her he acted like this, but before! How often in the past had she hungered for a kind word from him, or a tender glance, and nearly been driven crazy by his silence and coldness. No, she didn't care a bit that the baby was not his.

'You knew very well how happy it would make me, my dear,' Gerner continued. '*That*'s been the flaw in our marriage – that no children have come.'

'But I don't have the slightest interest in having a child!' She sent the teaspoon with which she had been tracing lines on the tablecloth clanking against the cup. 'You'll just bring it up to be scornful and horrid to me, the way you treat me yourself.'

'Really, Lucie,' he spoke in a mildly reproachful tone. 'It's not good for you to get so worked up in your condition. Some time you really must learn that you have certain duties.'

'Ha, ha, ha! I don't give a hoot about your duties! I don't suppose you had any duties to me.' She stretched her arms across the table and swung her head back and forth. 'You took me for your wife, you did do that, but how have you treated me? Like someone unspeakable. – And what right did you have. As if all you men aren't unspeakable! Now this is what you get, this is what you get! You're happy about the baby? Ha, ha, ha! Be happy all you want!' She was utterly beside herself, her face ugly and contorted.

Gerner's half-closed eyes flickered open and he stared at her. He was worried about her sanity. He had never seen her like this before.

'It's the plebian blood,' he muttered through clenched teeth. Although vaguely fearful of upsetting her more, he couldn't resist saying in a cold, scornful tone, 'Is it common for a woman to act so abnormally when she is with child?'

'Oh yes, throw it in my face that this has happened before!' Lucie cried in a shrill voice, laughing with pleasure at uttering the worst things she could think of. 'But that time I wasn't like this at all, because he – the man I was engaged to – loved me, and he treated me like a queen, I'll have you know. That's the difference!'

Gerner was dumbfounded for a moment. His face darkened and he gasped for air. Then he tore off his napkin, wadded it up, and threw it down on the table.

'Engaged… you?' he snarled, getting up and violently shoving his chair back in.

He walked out of the room with hurried steps. A moment later, Lucie heard him slam the front door and go down the stairs.

When Gerner came home late that night, Lucie was sleeping soundly.

He wasn't angry any longer. It was his duty now to tolerate

everything for the sake of the child on the way. Pregnant women were hard to figure out. Many went completely insane. Things would straighten out after the crisis had passed. It would be an ordeal in the meantime, but he would have to bear that.

He leaned over the bed and looked at Lucie. Her half-open lips had a tired and bitter expression and there was a crease between her eyebrows that he had not seen before. Through an opening in her nightgown her full white breasts were visible. They softly rose with every breath.

He was moved by the thought that she was sleeping with his child beneath her heart. This beautiful, lush body was his possession, and it had belonged only to him for over four years. And now she was bringing his child into the world. At last.

He bent down even closer and was about to kiss her. But then he stopped himself. Suppose she woke up; she mustn't know about his weakness. He was at least due an apology for her ugly behaviour. Otherwise she would be completely corrupted.

But the urge to kiss her had awakened memories of the old days, when he had a key to her door and often came up in the middle of the night and woke her with a kiss. So many delightful memories had been shared with her. And there was all the joy and pleasure she had given him. It was true that he had been too strict and unyielding with her. He remembered all the times when she had lain at his feet, sobbing her heart out, begging him to speak to her. But that was a long time ago. She had become very different.

He straightened up from the bed with a deep sigh. And then the nagging feeling that he had wronged her rose in him again, as it often had before. It was like being poked in a tender spot in his chest.

XX
Conversion

Knut had racked his brain for ways to prevent Lucie's hypnosis-induced visit, for he was fully convinced that she would come.

After making and abandoning a number of different plans, he finally made a decision, which also won Henny's approval, to visit her on Friday afternoon and speak to her.

An hour after Theodor had gone to the office, Lucie heard the doorbell ring. Unaccustomed to receiving visitors, especially at this time of day, she remained calmly sitting by the open window of the sitting room, her cheek propped on her hand, her elbow on the windowsill.

She looked limp and depressed. Her dry lips were covered with a yellowish film and her tired eyes stared absently at the chestnut tree and the half-shrivelled laburnum bushes in the neighbour's yard across the way. Her breathing was shallow and laboured and she had opened the buttons of her bodice so her corset was visible under her breasts.

'There's a gentleman asking for you, madam, if you please.'

Lucie took the card Martine handed to her and read: Knut Reinertson, First Lieutenant.

She blushed, put her hand to her hair, and said, 'Show him in. Tell him I'll be back in a moment.'

She was already on the way to the bedroom, where she fastened her dress while she held her breath, ran her fingers through the front of her hair, and powdered her blotchy cheeks. On the way back to the sitting room, she bit her lips to make them pink. Her heart was pounding and her hands shook.

'Good day, Lieutenant Reinertson! How nice of you to come calling in this stifling summer heat.' She held out both hands to him.

He had planned to be considerate and gentle and try not to hurt her too much. But now there was something so provocatively obliging about her. And the truth is, she's quite ugly, he thought. Dammit!

'Actually, I just have a message for you, Mrs. Gerner,' he said with a stiff bow.

Ignoring his cold tone, she went on, as she seized his hand and shook it, 'It's so very strange, too. Just today, I've been thinking about you so much.'

'That's just what I was afraid of,' he answered in his clear, strong voice. 'And that's why I thought I had better come up here.'

'Do you want to hear something odd?' She smiled at him and narrowed her eyes. 'I had got the idea of coming to see you, what do you think of that! Ullevålsveien, number 34, second floor. How I know you live *there* I have no idea, but I know that I know it. My goodness, you're completely crazy, I told myself, and that's what myself thought too. – But Lord knows if I wouldn't have come just the same. But won't you sit down? Oh yes, do.' She pushed a chair in his direction and sat down facing him.

'Thanks, but I'll be leaving soon,' he said dismissively, but sat down anyway. In one hand he was holding his cap, the other hand was resting on the hilt of his sword. 'Anyhow, I just came to apologise for the last time we were together.'

'Don't mention it,' Lucie said hurriedly, with a movement of her head and hands that suggested she was recollecting an amusing prank. 'Down there on the terrace – we'll forget about that.'

'You remember that I hypnotised you out on Malmø.'

'I certainly do remember,' she interrupted, pretending to shiver. 'Brrr!'

'Well, you don't know that during the time you were asleep, before Aunt Reinertson and Miss Brandt came in again, I ordered you to come visit me tonight at exactly 7:00, and I told you where I live.'

'No, for heaven's sake! Why did you do *that*, Lieutenant Reinertson? That must be why I thought I absolutely had to come and see you tonight. What made you do that?'

'It was a foolish prank, a confounded stupid impulse! I've regretted it very much ever since, and I beg you not to be angry and not to tell anybody about it.' He stood up.

Disappointed and humiliated, but unwilling to let herself show it, Lucie laughed nervously and said, 'Well I guess I'll have to forgive you, although you certainly don't deserve it. But won't you sit down? There's not any rush, is there?' She lightly touched his arm. 'We can still have a little chat, can't we?'

'I don't have time, Mrs. Gerner. My fiancée is expecting me.'

'What! You're engaged?' Her voice suddenly sounded sharp and off key.

'Yes, but it won't be announced for a couple of days. Then I'll have the honour of sending you a card.'

His glowing expression when he said 'my fiancée' had wounded Lucie. She thought of the scene in Mrs. Reinertson's garden and of the things she had imagined when he came in. A bitter shame seized her. A large round cloudy patch appeared before her eyes. The painting on the wall glided away and became a dot. Then it divided and became three and then became one again. Lord God, how he must despise her.

'Of course you knew I was just joking, didn't you?' she said in confusion, giving him a forced smile. 'Imagine *me* going to see you! Not for all the world.'

He bowed and gave a little salute. 'It's good that we agree, Mrs. Gerner,' he said and walked to the door.

Her gaze followed him, resting on his straight back and broad shoulders, his thick curly hair that grew to a point on his tanned, beautiful neck; and a searing envy of the woman who would have him flashed through her.

Without looking back, he left the room.

'Why should he care about me, the Tivoli-wife, carpenter Rasmussen's daughter, a former theatre walk-on, when he can use me any way he wants, any time he feels like it. I'm in the same situation as a man. – The ones who want to flirt with me have no qualms about taking liberties, and if I tried to be virtuous, they'd probably laugh in my face – like streetwalkers when they meet a virtuous man. Men and a woman like me can never be virtuous. In the first place, nobody expects it, and second, we can't shake our old habits.'

She sat down in her former position by the window and looked at the neighbour's garden. Now with the sun gone and the leaves on the trees grey and dusty, everything looked so blighted. The garden reminded her of the corner of the churchyard where her sisters were buried down in Kragerø. Oh she wished she were lying there, too. The world was so bitter and full of thorns, and human beings were false and lustful. Big tears trickled slowly down her cheeks.

That lieutenant – he'd only wanted to flirt with her because of the way she'd been before, and that's why he thought he could behave like that with her. But oh how sweet and handsome he was! She would have loved him in a very different way than his fine fiancée – whoever she was – if only he'd wanted that. But he didn't want it.

Oh, that garden over there reminded her so much of the churchyard where her sisters lay. Her sisters were in Heaven now, for there *was* a Heaven, there *must be* a Heaven. It didn't matter what they said, or what it said in books. Our life on earth was too horrid for there not to be a better world to come. Like now, when you saw how everything was going wrong. – Oh that sweet, sweet Lieutenant Reinertson. If he had loved her, she would have run away with him, and afterwards, when they didn't have anything to live on, she'd have killed herself for his sake. Yes, that's what she would have done. Then this untimely foetus she was carrying wouldn't be born either.

No, turn to the Lord. The way was simple enough: you just had to believe that Jesus had redeemed you. She drifted into a pious mood that relieved and moved her. When it was time for her to deliver, she would surely die, and that was what she wanted. If only she could be well prepared. Turn to the Lord and say goodbye to the vanity of the world. They could have the world, if that's what they wanted, as for her, she'd had quite enough of it.

If only she could stop thinking about Lieutenant Reinertson's beautiful neck. How strange – he'd been so captivated by *her* neck. The way he kissed her; she shivered voluptuously. – But he hadn't meant anything by it, of course.

No, turn to the Lord. That was the only thing left.

If she could still feel the way she did that time in Kragerø, when she went to prayer meetings with Mortensen and wept over her sins as if she was being whipped. She'd been happy then, because she felt like she was a child of God. If only she'd continued that way and not let herself be drawn into sin again, things would have gone much better for her, even if she had been the poorest and most wretched of the poor, for what does it benefit a man if he gains the world and loses his soul. – Oh how often Mortensen had preached about those verses. Then maybe she might have travelled to the Zulu mission, like Lina did. *She* had a true conversion, even though she'd gone just as far astray, although she didn't have as many temptations because she wasn't as beautiful. Being beautiful was a great danger and temptation. If only she had been ugly, so nobody would have looked at her twice. Or else been well born. For what had it brought her? Misery and misfortune from every direction. And she was so sinful. There wasn't a single particle of her that was pure, not *one* single particle.

What Mrs. Reinertson said was all rubbish! What did it have to do with this world? And wasn't what happened here and now the most important thing?

Turn to the Lord. Surely she could still be forgiven, when she had converted. And the lieutenant, so painfully handsome in her memory – she ought to be able to forget him.

'Help me! Help me, dear God in Heaven!' she cried out loud. 'Don't you see how I weep and implore you? Don't you see how the tears are streaming from my eyes, just like the repentant sinner I read about with the pastor? From now on, I won't think about anything except my conversion. Get out the Bible, starting right now.

Oh what joy to Jesus you would bring,
If his praises now you start to sing.

She walked over to the bookcase and took out the New Testament. 'Read about the repentant sinner and how blessed it is to belong to the Lord.

'If I can only find it.' She sat down on the sofa and leafed through the New Testament until she found the headings she was searching for in Luke:

> Jesus heals a centurion's servant, 1-10; raises a widow's son from the dead, 11-17; reveals himself to the disciples of John the Baptist, 18-23; speaks to the people about John and their lack of faith, 24—35; justifies himself and comforts a woman who has sinned.

She read the chapter through and when she came to the story of the woman who fell weeping at His feet, her face twitched and the tears rolled down her cheeks and fell onto the book. Oh, if this was still the time when Jesus walked the earth among us, and He had appeared before her. She would have thrown herself down before Him and bathed His feet with her tears, dried them with her hair and kissed them, and He would have said to her, 'Thy sins are forgiven. Thy faith hath saved thee; go in peace.'

For Lucie, it was as if the image of Lieutenant Reinertson suddenly flew away, far away, and disappeared. 'Dear God, I thank you!' she cried, sliding onto her knees, her elbows on the sofa and her face in her hands. 'Satan has left me.'

'Thy sins are forgiven; go in peace.' To this very day, these were words Jesus said to all who repented and were born again. Imagine knowing in your heart that sin had been lifted from you, and that in God's eyes, you were like someone who had never sinned. If she could only be convinced of this in her heart, then she would certainly not care about how Theodor behaved or about what Lieutenant Reinertson thought of her. And then possibly the Lord would be merciful enough to not let that filthy tramp out in the fields be the one who had made her pregnant. For God, the all-knowing, must have known beforehand that she would be converted, and then He wouldn't have the heart to do that. For her to have to look at a strange man's child would be a punishment and curse for her sinful life, and then she wouldn't have the courage to believe she was forgiven. But

God wouldn't let that happen now. He could do anything, even perform miracles. She would go to church every Sunday, and to prayer meetings, and read pious books. She wouldn't think about anything but what belonged to the Kingdom of God, the entire time she was in this condition. Perhaps then she could also get Theodor to convert. Our Lord would be pleased about that, and credit it to her account.

XXI
Waiting

One evening a couple of months later, Mørk and Gerner were walking together up Karl Johan.

'Well, how are things going at home these days,' Mørk asked.

'Not so well,' Gerner replied. 'She suffers from headaches and toothaches.'

'And her appetite?'

'Her appetite is good.'

'That's the most important thing. Just see that you keep her spirits up.'

'How do you keep the spirits up of someone who does nothing but read the Bible and prayer books from morning to night, weeping and talking about death and the time of our visitation. I'm really at my wits' end with her.'

'Just say yes to everything. The worst thing you can do is disagree with her. It's very common for them to have spells like this. When the whole business is over, *this* will be over too.'

'And then she's running to church every single Sunday. Twice in a row, she's become ill during the sermon. I've literally had to drag her out. What a disgraceful scene, and I don't dare let her go by herself either.'

'Well it's no easy matter. Indeed it isn't. But she'll soon be so uncomfortable that it will be impossible.'

'She won't give in,' Gerner said with a sigh. 'Every other night at least, she's at Bible lessons or prayer meetings. How she gets there I don't know, because at home she can barely drag herself from one room to the next. – Her legs are as thick as posts.'

'Well just take it easy, Gerner, old boy.' Mørk stopped at the corner of Universitetsgaten and shook Gerner's hand. 'Good-bye, then! Only two months to go now.'

'Did madam leave very long ago?' Gerner asked. He had come home and seen that Lucie was gone.

'It was around 6:30,' answered Martine, who was setting the supper table.

Shortly afterwards Lucie came in. She went into the dining room, rang for Martine, and let her pull off her boots and put on her slippers. Then she lay back in the chaise longue in the corner, where she usually spent most of the day.

Martine lit a lamp with a shade and placed it on the little table in front of the chaise longue.

Reaching under an embroidered pillow, Lucie pulled out a little black cloth book with gilt letters on the cover, and began to read.

Gerner came in and sat down on a chair beside the chaise longue. 'Where have you been this evening?'

'You know perfectly well that I never go out any place except where I can hear God's word,' Lucie answered, her tear-reddened eyes fastened on the book.

'Yes, but where, I meant – to the gymnastics hall?'

'No, the mission house.'

'Who was speaking?'

'Dønnergaard.'

'You do know that Mørk has forbidden you to go where there are so many people, Lucie.'

'We should obey God rather than man.'

Gerner made an impatient movement and mumbled, 'Well, there are all sorts of ways.'

'You can forbid everything else,' Lucie said with a martyred expression. 'I can bear that, because I'm used to it. But you can't keep me from seeking the Lord. It's disgraceful enough that you won't reflect on these things yourself, without dragging me away from it too.'

'But when it makes you ill, Lucie? Think of your headaches and dizziness.'

'What does it matter if this wretched body perishes as long as the soul is saved? You should have heard how beautifully he spoke tonight. If you had been there, maybe it would have touched you too, even as hardened as you are.'

Gerner leaned forward in the chair, with his elbows resting on his legs and his hands clasped between his knees.

'Listen to what St. Thomas à Kempis says,' Lucie continued.

> Being subjected to the necessity of eating and drinking, waking and sleeping, physical rest and work, and the remaining requirements of nature, is, in truth, a great burden and an agony to the pious soul, who yearns to be perfect and free from all sin.

'You've really got to stop this foolishness,' Gerner said, his shoulders twitching.

'Wait until the moment of death comes and you stand at the foot of God's throne. On the day of judgement, human beings will have to account for every wrongful word they have spoken. I don't think you're going to be so cocky then, Theodor, old boy – and I'll tell you this – not for all the splendours in the world would I exchange *my* condition for *yours*.'

'I bought a cradle today,' Gerner said after a little bit. 'A quite sweet little thing, blue embroidered coverlet, blue curtains and a sheet trimmed with lace. – I think I got it for a good price.'

'Am I supposed to look at that monstrosity from now on?' Lucie said fretfully. 'Just so I know I have something to look forward to. I really think there'll be plenty of time for that.'

'It can stay down there in the meantime. I told them they would get further instructions about where and when to deliver it.'

'Then I think they'll swindle you for sure. They'd be really stupid not to give you a piece of trash instead of the one you picked out.'

Theodor sighed and said nothing.

'Shouldn't you start thinking about baby clothes soon?' he said after a pause. 'It won't do to put it off any longer, Lucie. Today is the first of October.'

'There's no hurry,' Lucie said obstinately.

'Would you let me take care of it?'

'Could you do it? A man?'

'I'll ask Mrs. Reinertson to help me. Or Mrs. Mørk perhaps.'

'Yes, if you want,' she said indifferently. 'It makes no difference to me who does it. I'll have nothing to do with it anyway, because I'm going to die. I'm sure of it.'

Lucie had often said this in recent days, and each time she had noticed that it made an impression on Theodor. Today, however, he seemed unmoved by her words.

'Think how good it will be for you, Theodor, when I'm in my grave,' Lucie continued in a tone that sounded as if she were sincerely happy on his behalf. 'You'll be relieved, I think.'

It was a moment before he straightened up from his bowed posture and said mildly, 'No, Lucie, that wouldn't be good for me. I want you to live very much, so I can show you how I would treat you. I have not always acted the way I should.'

Lucie felt a sudden flash of emotion. This was the first time in their marriage that Theodor had admitted that he had not acted the way he should. She nearly held her arms up to him, but then she felt embarrassed and refrained.

Gerner stood up and stroked her hair, then sat down at the supper table.

Martine came in with a tray of sandwiches and a pitcher of milk, which she placed on the table in front of Lucie. They ate in silence.

Later when they were going to bed, Gerner helped Lucie up from the chaise longue. Slowly, supporting herself on his arm, she dragged herself into the bedroom. When she had taken off her dress and petticoats, Gerner kneeled down and pulled off her stockings. She was so heavy that she couldn't bend over.

During the night, Gerner was awakened by Lucie sitting bolt upright, sobbing convulsively, and striking out with her arms. She was talking about a deformed baby with brown spots over its whole body, and screaming for them to take it away.

'Wake up, Lucie,' said Gerner, taking hold of her arm. 'Remember, it's only a dream – that stupid, ugly dream you always have. Now, now, lie down and go back to sleep.'

Finally he settled her down. She turned her head away and looked at the little night lamp over on the dressing table.

Then her mind filled with the thoughts that never left her: Would the baby have a brown birthmark with long hair on its cheek beneath its left eye, or would it not?

Oh she was going to dread seeing the baby after it was born. She wouldn't ask, just wait until the midwife laid it in her arms. She could restrain herself that long. But then, what if it… She shuddered.

But she had begged and pleaded with God not to let that happen. Sometimes she felt certain that God had answered her prayers. And that would mean that the child was Theodor's and that our Lord had forgiven all her sins. But then at other times, and more frequently, she was sure that the birthmark was going to be there – big and brown and disgusting, with long black hair.

XXII
Ending

Gerner paced back and forth in his room. The room was half dark although it was late in the morning. Outside the November fog was heavy, grey and unmoving, and the stove would not draw. Dirty, dust-saturated moisture covered the outside of the windows, and the houses across the way were indistinguishable.

Gerner looked pale and exhausted. His eyes were strained and red-rimmed and his long white fingers fiddled nervously with his watch chain.

Every so often a muffled groan penetrated the room. Then he stopped and listened intently with his head bowed and his eyes staring at the rug.

Lucie's labour pains had begun at 4:00 in the morning. At 7:00, Gerner had gone to fetch the midwife and the maid who would care for Lucie while she was confined to bed.

He considered whether he should go to the office for a while. It was so terrible to be here at home and not dare to go in to see Lucie, for she had angrily and emphatically declared that he couldn't come in. He couldn't forget the expression and voice in which she shouted: 'Get out! Get out!' when he had ventured in there an hour ago.

He tiptoed through the dining room into the back hall and opened the kitchen door.

A thin little woman with a cap on her head and her hands folded outside her large rumpled apron was sitting on a chair close to the stove, where a large pot of water was heating. In front of the kitchen table, Martine stood peeling potatoes.

'Oh, Mrs. Halvorsen, may I have a word?'

The woman rose and came over to Gerner in a quick, obliging way.

'I would like to speak with the midwife for a second,' Gerner whispered, tilting his head in the direction of the bedroom. A wail of misery that turned into piercing sobs forced its way out to them. Gerner squeezed his eyes shut. 'Oh God, oh God, I'm dying Mrs. Sæby. I'm dying!' The cry ended in a drawn-out wimpering sigh, and then it was still.

Gerner waited a little, his fingers clamped tightly on the handle of the kitchen door, which he was holding ajar. The little woman stood in front of him with downcast eyes and a pious expression. Martine continued her work undisturbed.

'Ask the midwife to come into the dining room for a moment.' He made space for the woman to slip past him. 'Shh, shh, as quietly as possible.' He went into the dining room and carefully closed the door behind him.

In a short while a tall woman appeared wearing a brown woollen dress that looked like it was hanging on a stick. She held her head cocked to one side, tilted down slightly, and she looked up with strange furtive eyes that were dull and lively at the same time. Her unkempt hair was carelessly arranged in a thin bun in back. Her mouth, wide and thin, with spaces between her teeth, seemed so accustomed to smile and grimace that it couldn't be still for a moment.

'How is she doing?' Gerner whispered.

'Everything's just fine,' Mrs. Sæby lisped. 'The missus is so patient. With Jesus's help, everything will go as it should.'

Although she spoke in a muffled, dried-up voice, with her head constantly drooping at an angle, there was something so astonishingly mobile about her play of expression and her way of using her long pointed tongue that it had a jarring effect.

'I should go down to the office,' Gerner said. 'But I'd hate to… do you think it will be much longer?'

'Heavens yes!' She made a limp movement of her dark rubbery hands, which she clasped tightly against her breast, rubbing one hand continously over the other. 'It's going to be a long while yet. These are just little ones, Mr. Gerner sir. Nothing serious will happen here until this afternoon. Heavens yes, go ahead. Our Lord will stay here.'

Another wail came from the bedroom, and quickly, without a sound, the midwife went inside.

Gerner was detained at the office longer than he had intended. Every time he got ready to leave, somebody came who wanted to talk to him. Although he had the greatest difficulty keeping his thoughts collected, there was actually a kind of relief in listening to talk about lawsuits and house mortgages, all the while saying over and over to himself: 'Then it will be over when I get there.'

Sometime around 3:00 he was hanging his hat and coat in the hallway at home when a scream reached him that was unrecognizable as human. It sliced through the air, so wild and maddened, so shrill and uncontrollable that his limbs stiffened in terror. After a few seconds, it stopped. Then there was the sound of doors and hurried steps.

Gerner sneaked into the dining room. A voice in the back hall said something, but it couldn't have been Mrs. Halvorsen because it sounded so happy and loud. Martine answered, 'Well God be praised!'

Then came the laboured footsteps of someone carrying something, and Martine spoke again, 'Don't you want me to help you with that wash tub, Mrs. Halvorsen?' The footsteps went into the bedroom from the door in the back hall and something heavy was set down on the floor.

Gerner slipped over to the bedroom door and listened.

He heard the sound of a smack on a naked body. Then Mrs. Sæby's dry voice, 'He's taking his time about it.' Then another smack, followed by a frail, prolonged baby's cry.

Gerner clasped his head in his hands, leaned against the door and wept.

In a little while he straightened up, sat down carefully on a chair nearby and made an effort to follow what was happening inside.

As the baby continued to wail, he heard the trickle and splash of water. 'So big and healthy,' Mrs. Halvorsen's voice said – 'such a fat body and what a head. No wonder it was so hard on her. Hand me that wool blanket over there!'

Then came the sound of water. The baby's crying stopped and he could hear only a quiet puttering about and an affectionate drawling voice, 'So dear and sweet – Lordy, what a big boy he is, so healthy and plump.'

He couldn't stand it any longer. He had to go in. Three times he placed his hand on the door handle, but let go of it again. Finally, the fourth time, he gathered his courage and went in so quietly that nobody heard a thing.

The only light in the room came from the dull glass shade of a lamp on the washstand. In front of the large folding screen that hid the bed, Mrs. Halvorsen was sitting on a footstool with the baby, swaddling it on her lap. A white wool blanket hung down over her knees and lay on the floor around her.

Gerner walked over to the folding screen and stuck his head inside.

Lucie was lying there white-faced, with pale lips and closed eyes. Mrs. Sæby straightened her top sheet and wrapped the blanket tightly around her. Then she took first one arm and then the other, and made them into a circle so that her hands met on top of the blanket.

'There, in Jesus's name,' she said, straightening up, 'now the missus can just relax.'

'Everything went so naturally and well,' she turned to Gerner, who had stepped behind the folding screen. 'Quite according to nature. Thank the Lord. You can never marvel enough at our allmighty Lord's miracles.'

Gerner walked over to the bed, took Lucie's hand and kissed it. She opened her eyes but immediately closed them again.

Then he bent down and kissed her forehead. 'My poor Lucie,' he whispered. 'Thank God it's over.'

Lucie didn't move.

Gerner went around to the other side of the folding screen. 'Was it difficult?' he asked.

'It was no child's play, sir,' answered Mrs. Sæby, with her jarring smile. 'Such a giant of a boy!' She pointed to the baby. 'I'm sure he weighs at least six kilos. And so like his father. – That fellow won't have to make up any stories about who his father is.'

Gerner bent over Mrs. Halvorsen's lap and looked at the baby's little red face. 'Very big head,' he said.

'You've never seen the like, sir,' answered Mrs. Sæby, touching the unusually protruding back of the baby's head. 'A real pastor's head.'

'Hasn't he got an unusual amount of hair?' Gerner asked, cautiously running his fingers over the baby's head.

'Oh yes! Lovely brown curly hair – shh – I think the missus is saying something.' The midwife slipped quickly past the folding screen.

'Show it to me,' Lucie whispered, without opening her eyes.

The midwife picked up the baby and carried it over to Lucie.

'It's best if we put it to the breast right away,' she said coaxingly. 'That will be so good and helpful for the missus.'

'I want to look at it,' Lucie said with a listless, dismissive movement of her hand.

The midwife held the baby so she could see the right side of his face.

'Turn it,' Lucie said. Her eyes were wide open and looked as round as saucers.

Madam Sæby did as she was told.

Lucie saw a little brown birthmark with soft dark hair on the left cheek directly under the eye.

'Take it away! Away!' Lucie screamed, wildly flailing her arms. Her face had become dark grey and rigid.

Then she had a fit of hysterical laughter that lasted over an hour.

The doctor was summoned in the meantime.

The laughter was followed by a hysterical fit of weeping, so violent and continuous that it seemed as if her body would be shaken to pieces. She sat bolt upright and tried to get out of bed, and when they forcibly restrained her, she thrashed about like a madwoman.

Mørk gave orders to find a wet nurse.

Then the fever began.

She lay there with an ice bag on her head. Her eyes glittered, the skin on her lips was brown and encrusted with bloody marks from when she bit them during her fit, and her sunken cheeks were unnaturally pink. She talked and gesticulated continuously and was never in her right mind for a moment.

'It's the morphine,' Mørk said, 'but it takes the pain away.'

As he sat by the bed during the long, long hours when he was taking the night nurse's place, Gerner thought of their life together, especially before she became his wife.

A couple of times a night he tiptoed into the dining room, which had been converted to a nursery, and stood for a long time over the cradle, where the baby lay breathing with his nose pressed against the pillow and his little cheek turned up, pink and warm. Then tears came to his eyes and his stiff, hopeless face became soft and troubled. 'My poor little mite,' he mumbled again and again, as he lightly brushed the child's head with his lips.

'Get away from me! Get away, I tell you!' Lucie would cry occasionally, sitting bolt upright. 'You smell horrible, and those rough filthy clothes! – I'm a fine lady. And my husband is a lawyer. – That disgusting brown birthmark. – Oh no, don't kill me! Don't kill me – I'll lie as quiet as a mouse, you'll see. – Ugh, ugh, those hairs are so nasty – oh help me, help me!' She flailed her arms in the air and clutched at her husband's hands, which were always there, gripped them so hard that her nails dug into his fingers.

Then she crouched in the bed with her legs drawn up beneath her, gripped him by the neck and said with terrible staring eyes, 'Is that you, Theodor? You're the worst, the most rotten of all of them – a disgusting whore-monger. You're much, much worse than I've ever been.'

Then she would fall back on the pillow and weep streams of tears, chattering incessantly into the air.

And all through it, Gerner was changing the ice pack on her head, giving her medicine, straightening the pillow, and pulling the blanket up around her as tears trickled down his cheeks.

On the evening of the fourth day, the doctors said all hope was gone.

Gerner sat by the bed keeping watch over Lucie hour after hour. She had lain in a doze since nine o'clock in the evening. With the big white ice bag that looked like a turban and her glowing pink cheeks, she looked like a complete stranger. Occasionally from the dining room came the sound of the baby whimpering and fretting, but Lucie didn't hear it. She lay without moving. Her breast heaved convulsively for each breath. Once in a while she lifted her arm and moved her hand back and forth; then it fell heavily again.

Gerner had completely accepted the fact that she was going to die, and a dull calm had come over him. He thought about everything that had happened between them, from that first night, when he had pursued her after the show at Tivoli, up to the day she had the baby. He went through all of it, piece by piece, link by link. He came to the conclusion that he had nothing to reproach himself for. He had been an honourable husband to her. Because he was so in love with her that he couldn't live without her, he had made her his wife, and he had faithfully and energetically striven to make their marriage succeed. That it hadn't been more successful was not his fault, but partly her own, partly something stronger than himself – his inability to forget her past. Suddenly he remembered the words Lucie had spoken the night she came back from Malmø. 'You treat me like someone unspeakable, but what right do you have? All you men…'

He jumped up when Lucie raised herself in the bed and moved her right arm as if she were beckoning to someone.

'What is it Lucie darling, my sweet Lucie, what is it?'

He took her burning dry hand.

'It has to drive closer,' Lucie said in a low, but strangely distinct voice, 'all the way over so we can get in from here. Mrs. Reinertson and I will ride inside, and the Lieutenant and Nilsa, too, but you have to ride up on the box, Theodor.' – She slowly turned her head and looked at him with dimming eyes, – 'I don't want you inside, Theodor. – No not that plain one, we'll take that fine funeral carriage. Gee-up, gee-up, gee-up.' She pursed her lips and tried to make a clucking sound. 'Drive on, drive on, what are you waiting for?' She sank back on the pillow, and Gerner thought it was all over, but in a few minutes she lifted herself again and said hoarsely to herself, 'He said it was my fault, but this ought to show him.' Then she laughed briefly and fell back on the pillow.

Immediately afterward, the death struggle began. Gerner poured

145

a dose of musk powder into her and held her head with both hands.

She lay still, her breath rattling in her throat, her fingers plucking at the covers.

Suddenly she reared up, grabbed Gerner by the arm, pressed her other hand to her heart, and with a convulsive movement of her whole body, vomited. It came with such force that it streamed over the bedclothes and onto the floor.

Then she fell back heavily. Her eyes rolled and her mouth worked. She lay quite still, breathing feebly, the intervals becoming longer and longer.

Then she stretched and was dead.

Footnotes (see * in text)

1) Chapter V (p.39)

The Gauntlet (*En Handske*), a controversial play by Norwegian author and cultural leader Bjørnstjerne Bjørnson (1832-1910). Attacking the double standard, Bjørnson declared that both men and women should remain chaste before marriage; the play was the impetus to a heated debate that became known as the Great Scandinavian Morality Debate. See Afterword for further discussion.

2) Chapter VI (p.47)

Albertine, a novel by the well-known Norwegian painter Christian Krohg (1852-1925)). The story of a young seamstress who is driven to prostitution by poverty. See the Afterword for further discussion of the book.

3) Chapter XIV (p.90)

Gluntarne, a collection of 29 duets for baritone and bass depicting student life at Uppsala University in the 1840s; text and music by Gunnar Wennerberg (1817-1901).

4) Chapter XV (p.98)

The Commodore's Daughters, (*Kommandørens Døtre*) a novel by Norwegian author Jonas Lie (1833-1908), an important literary figure whose works were known throughout northern Europe at the end of the 19th century. In this novel and others Lie voices feminist sympathies.

5) Chapter XV (p.99)

'My Dear Old Mother,' (Du gamle mor), a poem by the Norwegian poet and journalist Aasmund Olafsson Vinje (1818-1870). Composer Edvard Grieg (1843-1907) set many of Vinje's lyrics to music.

Afterword

'I've been through a period of unpleasantness and adversity.
I had written a novel, Lucie, and couldn't get Salmonsen to
publish it. He was afraid of the content. So I sank into
despondency for months and thought my time was past; I took
out old linen and table cloths and sat mending and darning,
and got more grey hairs than I already had.'

Amalie Skram to Sophus Schandorph
31 July 1888

In 1888, the year she wrote *Lucie*, Amalie Skram was forty-two
years old. She had been living in Copenhagen for four years with her
second husband, Danish author and critic Erik Skram, and was
known for her frank and controversial writings in literary circles
throughout Scandinavia. Since the appearance of her first novel in
1885 Skram had published three novels but, remarkably, she did not
have a regular publisher. Her novels had been taken on commission
because no one had been willing to assume the financial risk of
publishing a woman who wrote controversial books. And now
publishers didn't even want to risk name association with *Lucie*, a
book that Skram admitted 'strikes right at all the uproar over the
morality debate.' Thanks to the intervention of Herman Bang, Skram
eventually did find a publisher for *Lucie* and for subsequent works.
But though *Lucie* received warm praise from some reviewers and
actually sold quite well, both novel and author were scorned in
conservative circles. They were outraged by Skram's portrayal of a
fallen woman who is victimised by bourgeois society. One year later,
in the spring of 1889, Amalie Skram's application for an artist's
stipend was refused by a government department in Kristiania
(present day Oslo), and the reason cited by one committee member
was Skram's authorship of *Lucie*. The novel shone too bright a light
on the social and sexual inequities in Norwegian society.

Amalie Skram's early years

Amalie Skram was uniquely positioned to tell the story of a lower-class woman who makes a providential marriage and learns the costs involved in crossing social boundaries. Born Berthe Amalie Alver in 1846, she spent her early life in Bergen, Norway. Her father was a shopkeeper, her mother a domestic servant, but they were enterprising and ambitious, and they sent Amalie and her brothers to the city's best grammar schools. In 1863 her father lost everything to risky business speculations. He left Norway for America and within months of his departure, when she was barely 18 years old, Amalie was engaged to marry a man of superior social standing, Captain August Müller. She accompanied Müller on his sailing trips visiting ports all over the world, and in 1871 the couple, by then the parents of two sons, settled in Bergen. The marriage disintegrated, and in 1877 Amalie Müller suffered a nervous breakdown brought on by her frustrated attempts to obtain a divorce from her husband. Ill and despairing, she was admitted to Gaustad Asylum in Kristiania. The doctor who treated her advised that her recovery necessitated separation from Müller, and after a three-month hospital stay, Amalie and her sons went to live with her brother in a small town south of Kristiania. There she cultivated the literary interests she had started to develop in Bergen, writing book reviews for the local newspaper and exchanging letters with authors she admired such as Bjørnstjerne Bjørnson and Georg Brandes. After three years in a small town, Amalie Müller was ready to move on to bigger things. In August 1881, together with her two boys, she went to live in the nation's capital, a city that was on the verge of revolt.

Scandinavian society in flux

The decade of the 1880s was a period of cultural turmoil and debate in Scandinavia. In Norway the uproar was political as well as cultural and social. By the early 1880s a liberal coalition of Norwegians had successfully challenged the King's right to exercise absolute veto. In 1814 Norway had formed a union with Sweden; the two countries were to share one king, King Karl Johan, and to be equal partners, but in reality Norway was the weaker member.

Norway's status had not been significantly altered in the ensuing decades, but now the liberals were sufficiently organised to fill the seats of the Storting (legislative body) and push for greater autonomy. Their ultimate goal was a form of government that was parliamentary and hence more democratic. This goal was finally accomplished in 1884 when the liberal party, Venstre, was invited by the King to form a government. But though the liberals had dealt the establishment a blow, they had not yet toppled it. The conservatives could still exert their power and influence and they used it to force the new government to make compromises that angered and disappointed their more radical constituents. Intellectuals, artists and authors who had been enthusiastic supporters of Venstre were now openly critical. And the issues that came to dominate their protest were social problems that had been brewing for some time: prostitution and sexual morality.

Prostitution had become a serious problem in Kristiania in the mid-nineteenth century as a result of the steady migration of the unemployed from the countryside to the city. Factories offered jobs, but not housing or other social benefits and wages were low. Workers built themselves simple houses on the periphery of the city centre, areas that soon developed into slums where brothels proliferated. Venereal disease was widespread among men and women of the lower class, but it also infiltrated the homes of the upper classes. In 1876 the authorities acknowledged the need to control the social disease with a series of regulations directed at the women who practiced prostitution (but not their male customers). Prostitutes were required to register and to report to the police station for a doctor's examination on a regular basis. They were not allowed to change residence without permission, attend concerts, visit restaurants, or take a tram. In short, they were discouraged from showing themselves in public spaces. Regulations notwithstanding, prostitution and venereal disease continued to flourish and in the early 1880s, at the time Amalie moved to the capital, the problem had become the topic of public debate.

The morality debate (sædelighedsdebatten)

In the autumn of 1881 Henrik Ibsen put venereal disease on the stage with his play *Ghosts* (*Gengangere*). In this 'family drama' a member of the establishment, Chamberlain Alving, contracts syphilis and then infects his family. Few theatres dared mount a production of *Ghosts*, and the play was savagely attacked in the press, even by liberal newspapers. Nonetheless, the stage had been set for the event often cited as the first volley in the public debate: a meeting of the Kristiania Workers' Society (Arbeidersamfund) in February 1882. This was the third in a series of meetings convened to discuss how to control prostitution in the city. Journalists were present so the lively discussion was reported in the newspapers. Many opinions and suggestions were aired: one man argued in favour of restricting the sale of alcohol, another favoured going after wealthy libertines who seduced working class girls, a third thought the answer lay in curbing people's animal desires. At the February meeting Hans Jæger took the floor and presented views that few of those present could condone. An unknown at the time, Jæger gained notoriety later in the decade as one of the leaders of the bohemian movement in Kristiania. In his opinion prostitution was the result of the institution of marriage and the wretched wages earned by female workers. Repressive attitudes about sex made it almost impossible for men to find sexual fulfillment in marriage, and so they went to lower class women who could not possibly live on the incomes earned from 'honest' work. At a subsequent meeting Jæger elaborated on his belief that true liberation could only be attained when society allowed both sexes to practice free love.

Hans Jæger had identified the double standard as the cause of society's ills and the cure he prescribed was pre- and extramarital sex for women as well as men. Quite predictably, the good people of Kristiania were scandalised. A year later Jæger's proposal was countered in a play by Bjørnstjerne Bjørnson, but the views he presented in *The Gauntlet* (*En Handske*, 1883) proved to be equally distasteful to the majority. Like Jæger, Bjørnson attacked the double standard of bourgeois marriage that demanded chastity from women yet condoned the sexual dalliances of men. But where Jæger called for sexual freedom for all, Bjørnson admonished men to be as innocent and pure as women before marriage and subsequently chaste and faithful husbands. *The Gauntlet* was mocked and derided by everyone except a small group of feminists, but Bjørnson's stature was such that even a poorly received play could succeed in fanning the flames of the public debate like nothing else.

The *Gauntlet* discussions in *Lucie* (chapters V, XIV and XVII) are a good reflection of the play's impact on conversations in bourgeois homes. Only Pastor Brandt argues for the position Bjørnson takes in *The Gauntlet* and even he is not consistent. For though he declares the play to be 'the greatest victory for Christianity we've had in a long time', he also defends male promiscuity as ordained in the Scriptures, citing 'examples from the Old Testament of patriarchs and others upon whom the Lord had bestowed innocent virgins so that they might enjoy them and beget offspring'. Clergymen in the State Church, incidentally, were generally not supporters of Bjørnson on this matter, reluctant as they were to relinquish male privilege. Bjørnson's call for universal chastity found more receptive ears in pietistic congregations where believers were admonished to shun all worldly pleasures. Pietism, a popular phenomenon in Norway during the second half of the nineteenth century, is also part of the background in Skram's novel, for it is to the Free Church, with its daily prayer meetings, that Lucie turns for solace and release.

Amalie Müller's years in Kristiania were exciting times and she followed the morality debate closely. She did not speak out at public meetings, but did let her views be known in review articles published in newspapers, although she didn't always sign her full name. A lengthy article defending and praising Ibsen's *Ghosts* was signed by 'ie'. She used her full name, Amalie Müller, when she wrote about *The Gauntlet* and in this case her enthusiasm was even warmer. 'It is our pride and our honour that in a time such as ours this demand has been made by our great national poet,' she wrote, and in correspondence from 1883 Amalie emphatically proclaimed Bjørnson a prophet. She was working on her first novel, *Constance Ring*, during this period, and the ideas and demands Bjørnson put forth in *The Gauntlet* were reflected in her own work. Constance has highly idealised notions about love, is sexually inexperienced and unable to accept the double standard practiced by all the men who court her.

Over the years Amalie's views on sexuality developed and changed. After her marriage to Erik Skram in 1884, married life in a new city, Copenhagen, amidst a new circle of friends undoubtedly influenced her thinking. The morality debate had heated up again with the appearance of two provocative books, Hans Jæger's *From the Kristiania Boheme* (*Fra Kristiania-Bohêmen*,1885) and Christian Krohg's *Albertine* (1886). *Albertine* made a particularly strong impression on Amalie Skram, and at the time she wrote *Lucie* in 1888 her position had shifted away from views Bjørnson expressed in *The Gauntlet*.

On the same day Jæger's *From the Kristiania Boheme* was published, 11 December 1885, it was confiscated by the vice unit under orders from the Department of Justice. Jæger was convicted of blasphemy and offending moral decency, fined and sentenced to 60 days in prison. A huge scandal followed. Jæger's supporters charged that the government had violated the Constitution of 1814 under which citizens are guaranteed freedom of speech; they felt betrayed by the liberal government and its leader, Johan Sverdrup. Jonas Lie and Arne Garborg were alone among Norway's authors to openly defend Jæger's right to be heard; artist Christian Krohg resolved to challenge the government action – and conservative opinion – by writing a novel about prostitution in Kristiania. His heroine is a young seamstress, Albertine, who lives and works in a poor section of town with her mother and brother. Krohg describes the slippery slope that ends in Albertine's prostitution, and delivers a scathing criticism of the police for their shameful treatment of women during mandatory visits to the police station for medical examinations. (Later Krohg depicted Albertine's story on canvas, and his painting, 'Albertine in the Police Doctor's Waiting Room', is prominently hung in the National Gallery in Oslo.) Krohg had intended to provoke the authorities with *Albertine* and his efforts were successful: *Albertine* was confiscated immediately upon publication (20 December 1886) and Krohg was fined 100 kroner. The public outcry was greater this time. Workers and students in Kristiania held meetings and demonstrations to protest the confiscation, and in Copenhagen Amalie Skram wrote a long article that was published in Norway as a pamphlet entitled *About Albertine* (Om Albertine) in 1887. Skram was deeply moved by Krohg's book and she made no attempt to conceal her emotion. She praised Krohg for the artistry of his novel – the characters were true-to-life, the descriptive passages painterly – and for the book's ethical content. The article opens with a warm and compassionate description of Albertine and her mother, good and honest people despite their poverty, and concludes with an impassioned defense of the rights of prostitutes. Those who read *Albertine*, Skram writes, will perhaps come away with an understanding that fallen women are human beings like themselves. And that may lead them to question why such women should be branded as whores and stripped of their civil rights. What about the men who go to them? Skram protests the different standards for men and women: 'The old drivel that says woman is such a delicate plant, that she suffers greater injury from overstepping the boundaries of chastity and morality has long since been found to be untenable.'

The first two volumes of Skram's naturalistic opus, *The People of Hellemyr* (*Hellemyrsfolket*) appeared in the autumn of 1887. It is easy to recognise the author of *The People of Hellemyr* in the pamphlet *About Albertine*. Both reflect the same compassion for people born in unfortunate circumstances, the same need to understand the social and personal forces that reduce people to abjection. Small wonder that Amalie Skram admired the work of Christian Krohg whose naturalistic paintings are the finest examples of that genre in Norwegian art. Yet Skram interrupted work on the third volume of *The People of Hellemyr* in order to write *Lucie*. Something in Krohg's book must have awakened the memory of a story crying to be told.

Amalie Skram and *Lucie*

Twice in letters to her friend Schandorph, Skram wrote that the material in Lucie was like a weight on her mind that gave her no peace; the subject 'wouldn't release me until I had put it down in black and white.' What was it about Lucie's story that affected her so powerfully? The answer seems to be both intellectual and emotional. As we have seen, Skram was passionately involved with the social and literary debates in Scandinavian society, and these controversies find their way into the political discussions among Lucie, the Reinertsons, and Pastor Brandt. Writing in Copenhagen, Skram recreated the varied social milieus of her former home in Kristiania; the city's streets, apartments, and tenements are described with almost sociological precision. But if *Lucie* is a faithful representation of the intellectual and social milieu of the time, it is also a personal novel. Amalie Skram had an unusual capacity to internalise the things she wrote about. She suffered along with her characters, and her emotional involvement suggests not only the vividness of her imagination but also a degree of identification. Skram did not share Lucie's sexual history, either in terms of experience or attitude. But like her heroine, she was a strikingly beautiful woman and she knew how female beauty affects not only the way a woman is regarded, but how she regards herself. Each woman came to Kristiania hoping to start a new life, yet each was indelibly marked by her past – Skram, a divorced woman who had spent time in a mental hospital, knew what it felt like to be an outsider. *Lucie* reflects Skram's empathy with women who were the casualties of bourgeois marriage, women who were sexually exploited or who had been ostracised from 'good' society because of their behaviour and background.

Lucie's society

As Irene Englestad points out,[i] *Lucie* depicts the values and attitudes of three social milieus: the lower-class Tivoli milieu of Nilsa and Olsen, the middle-class milieu of Gerner and the Mørks and the more bohemian milieu of Mrs. Reinertson and her family. Within each of these social spheres are different attitudes toward sexual experience in men and women, different ideals about social roles, and different ideas about marriage. In the Tivoli milieu, best exemplified in the chapter in which Lucie returns to Nilsa's apartment, men and women were equal – all poor and struggling to make a living – equally entitled to sexual freedom outside the boundaries of marriage. In Gerner's world, a world of secrecy and decorum, the double standard ruled: men were expected to have sexual experience, even keep a lower class 'bird in a cage', but the women they married were expected to have no 'stain'. In the Reinertsons' world, sexuality outside of marriage is freely discussed, and equality of sexual experience is considered just and appropriate. But even in the most liberal of the novel's environments the emotional responses to a woman's sexual experience lags behind the theoretical acceptance of it. Knut wants to marry Henny, even believing she has had lovers before, but he weeps in relief when he finds that her story is not true.

Amalie Skram's anger about the double standard and the sexual exploitation of women is as powerful a theme in *Lucie* as in *Constance Ring*. In the latter she shows how the sexual norms of her society constrain and deform the development of a middle-class woman like Constance. Lower-class women exist only in the background of the central plot – men use Kristine and Emma as sexual surrogates for women like Constance. In *Lucie*, Skram moves the lower-class girl to the foreground and reverses the roles between husband and wife. What happens within a marriage and within society if the wife has a sexually liberated past? Skram tracks Lucie as she moves from one milieu to the next, trying to pass, to model her behaviour on the women and men she encounters. But each of her efforts to cross a social boundary ends in a punishing encounter with male will: a judgmental husband, a careless roué, a brutal rapist, finally even an unresponsive Lord. However, *Lucie* is more than a demonstration of the inequities of the double standard, more than a tract about the various kinds of subjugations experienced by a lower-class woman in society. A schematic portrayal does not capture the power of the novel or address the reasons why it speaks to us today. In spite of its melodramatic elements, *Lucie* is a wrenching depiction of a marriage based on the expectation that personalities can be made anew. In their joint project to transform a Tivoli girl into a lady, Gerner and Lucie make their marriage into a prison. Skram does not limit her attention to Lucie's suffering. She shows Gerner's suffering too. The novel is a powerful psychological study of two characters trapped in a relationship from which they can't escape, in a world that constrains and punishes people when they cross rigid social boundaries.

Professor and pupil

Skram begins the novel in the 'professors' quarter,' an area near the university where Gerner has set Lucie up in an apartment that he visits nightly. The location of the love nest signals an important aspect of Lucie and Theodor's relationship. Gerner is one of the many learned doctors who populate nineteenth-century women's fiction. Descended from Charlotte Lenox's character in *The Female Quixote*,[ii] the learned doctor is a representative of community standards and expectations. His goal is to educate the heroine, to tame and socialise the wayward impulses of female mind and flesh. Lucie is a life force, sensuous, talkative, impulsive, constantly in motion. Gerner is the opposite: measured, constrained, timid, morbidly sensitive about other people's opinions. Like other learned doctors – Dr. Casaubon in *Middlemarch* comes to mind – Gerner is driven by both internal and external forces. In spite of his conventional exterior he is in thrall to his sexual passion for Lucie. Helpless to resist Lucie's attractions, he marries her to keep his sexual property away from other men. But he wants more than a beautiful woman whose sexuality is miraculously all for him. He has crossed a dangerous boundary by marrying Lucie, and he feels contaminated by his secret alliance with a fallen woman. On his nightly visits, he registers disgust at the dirty steps, the ugly courtyard, and the vulgar rooms in which he keeps Lucie.[iii] In order to cleanse both Lucie and himself, Gerner needs to obliterate Lucie's past identity: to that end he orders her not to have visits from her Tivoli friend Nilsa, to laugh quietly instead of 'whooping like a mule driver.' Even before they marry Gerner has begun his educational project.

At first Gerner has a willing pupil. Lucie has an aspiring mind; she believes in self-transformation. When the novel begins, she has already left several identities behind: firmly relegated to the past are her working class family, the ship's mate who seduced her, the baby who died at birth. Lucie has moved on, with scarcely a backward glance: 'Oh well. That was life. If she hadn't lost the baby she would never have met Theodor.' For Lucie, Theodor represents another chance to better herself – to leave her lover Olsen at Tivoli and become a new person, at first the mistress of a respectable man, and then, if the opportunity presents itself, his wife. Lucie thinks a new identity is as easy to put on as a new hat. 'Let's see how it looks on me,' she cries in the novel's first scene, eagerly seizing the fashionable new hat Nilsa brought her, then moving to a mirror to admire the effect. A beautiful blond girl stares back, confident that she is an object of male desire, aware that beauty is her primary currency. Later that evening Lucie returns to the mirror and approvingly examines her face, feature by feature, as if through Gerner's eyes. The chapter ends with a more explicit version of the earlier scene: Lucie, having deceived Gerner into proposing marriage, joyfully tries on her new identity for size: 'Mrs. Theodor Gerner, Mrs. Gerner, the lawyer's wife... Mrs. Lucie Gerner.' Instead of a secret life as a kept woman, she will now be able to walk down the public streets as the wife of a respectable man. Lucie will learn to become a lady and she understands her part of their marriage pact. She will submit to Gerner:

> Oh she would be so loving to him, would love him
> every day of the year, every hour of the day and submit
> herself to him. Yes, she would submit, no matter how he
> behaved, no matter how he treated her, for she really
> couldn't expect too much. And faithful! Oh so true to
> him – as good as gold. What bliss that would be.

Physical submission is easy for her. It will be more difficult to bend her mind and will to his.

In his role as a professor of middle-class deportment, Gerner calls to mind Bernard Shaw's learned doctor in *Pygmalion*.[iv] In the original Greek tale, a sculptor creates a statue of his ideal of womanly beauty and falls in love with it. Aphrodite takes pity on him and brings the statue to life. Skram makes use of the Pygmalion story in *Lucie*. Both Skram and Shaw portray men who wish to transform a living woman into perfection. Both works explore the unintended consequences of the transformation project. What happens when one person sets out to recreate another person? Shaw's essentially comic treatment gives Professor Higgins the task of creating a duchess out of a Covent Garden flower girl, and then explores the emotional consequences for each party. 'You have no idea how frightfully interesting it is to take a human being and change her into quite a different human being, by creating new speech for her,' Professor Higgins tells his mother. In spite of his intellectual and social superiority, he is blind to what his housekeeper sees immediately: 'You can't take a girl up like that, as if you were picking up a pebble at the beach.' Shaw shows Elisa's suffering, her sense that the transformation has made her unfit for any station in life. But there is a happy ending for Elisa; Shaw marries her not to the professor but to a suitable young man. In *Lucie,* Amalie Skram paints a darker picture: the efforts to recreate identity occur within a marriage. Blind to the hubris implicit in his project, Gerner wants to a create a new Lucie out of the old one, design a role for her and teach her how to play it. Just after the marriage, he tells his friend Mørk:

> She feels boundless gratitude toward me and is utterly dependent. I have so to speak created and invented her. She is young and soft as wax. I can make her into whatever I want.

But marriage teaches Gerner that the human personality is less pliable than wax. He does change Lucie, but his efforts at transformation create a character quite different than he imagined. In *Lucie*, Amalie Skram runs the Pygmalion story in reverse. The professor begins with a beautiful, vital woman and gradually strips her humanity away.

His teaching incomplete at the time of their marriage, Gerner intensifies his efforts when he moves Lucie out of the secret apartment into the broad daylight of his social circle. No behaviour is too insignificant for his critical attention. He uses every pedagogical weapon at his disposal – he lectures her on the inappropriateness of smiling too warmly when she is introduced to a man, of dancing too vigorously, of clinking glasses with their friends. Every sign of warmth or independent life becomes the occasion for a lecture. When lectures fail and Lucy ventures outside the boundaries he has set for her, he refuses to speak to her for days. Silence is his most painful method of instruction. She will behave like his creation or she will cease to exist for him. Yielding to his authority, Lucie tries valiantly to leave her old self behind. She wants to be made new, and she begs him to correct her behaviour, recognizing that she will not be able to rise in the world without his instruction. She weeps and begs forgiveness for her missteps. When she is sufficiently repentant, he confers forgiveness: 'Don't cry Lucie. There, now I recognise my old sweet Lucie again.' His ambivalence is clear; with all her faults, the 'old Lucie' was in some ways preferable – she was dependent, controllable, and eager to accept his teachings.

Gerner's jealousy

Behind Gerner's efforts to transform Lucie is his jealousy. Married to a woman with a past, he finds himself unable to forget her sexual history. Whenever Lucie is out on the street he is sure that men are approaching her. If she smiles at a man, he is sure that she knew him from before. He fears being disgraced and made ridiculous in the eyes of society. But underlying his jealousy is also a sense of inadequacy, his fear that she compares him with other more virile lovers from the past. Though both are sexually experienced, their experiences are not equal. Lucie has had at least two other lovers before Gerner, and borne a child by one of them. She was passionately in love with its father, and lived with Olsen during her time at Tivoli. In contrast, Gerner was married for a short time to a woman who had no 'stain' of sexuality about her. Lucie's free and easy sexuality has hit him like a bomb. All of his conservative moral views have been upended by his sexual passion for the beautiful blond dancer who has freely told him about her past. His mind has been poisoned by that knowledge:

> This frivolous tart that he had lifted out of filth and made his wife was setting herself against him. A woman who ought to be imbued with one single thought, one single goal, to erase the past, eternally on

guard to show him she had become a different person, to show him that not one drop of her blood yearned for anybody but him, desired anybody but him. She ought to be humble and repentant, a penitential Magdalene in mind and deportment. *Then* everything would be fine between them, because he really was in love with her. Yes, that was what was so painful, he was still in love with her.

His sexual insecurity is painfully obvious, even to himself, and it can only be relieved if Lucie becomes a different person, not the spontaneous, affectionate girl he married but a repentant sinner, a Magdalene who has left her sexual history behind.

Increasingly at cross purposes, Gerner and Lucie exist in the same house, but live in a kind of baffled fury about each other's recalcitrance. Gerner finds that the things that attracted him to Lucie are incompatible with her identity as his wife. He is annoyed by her hearty laugh and boisterous spirits. Her warm expressiveness now looks like immorality. Her efforts to model herself on Mrs. Reinertson seem like pretension. Rubbed raw by every sign of independent life, Gerner takes refuge in determinism. He bitterly reproaches Lucie for her 'plebian blood' and 'ill-bred defiance'. 'You're a tart, and you'll never get that out of your blood,' he tells her. Waiting for her to come home at night he broods about their relationship: 'You don't erase a past like that. Nothing can be erased. Everything, everything is subject to the law of necessity.' But his deterministic pronouncements are exculpatory. If character and identity are in the blood, he can't be blamed for failure. Lucie, in turn, has come to fear the very sight of him:

Now that he had educated her, he thought everything was fine, for he was quite merciful and kind to her now. But if he only knew how angry and bitter she felt toward him. Sometimes she felt like she could kill him just to get even. She wished to God she had never known or seen him.

Alienated from her life at Tivoli, alienated from her husband and his friends, Lucie can find no place where she feels at home. Matthew Arnold's poem describes her plight, Lucie is 'wandering between two worlds: one dead, one powerless to be born.'[v]

The meaning of sexual freedom

Lucie's history as a sexually liberated woman has different significance for each character. For Mrs. Mørk, Gerner's marriage to Lucie means that the couple is not welcome in her home. For Pastor Brandt, the social acceptance of a woman like Lucie means that the end of civilization is near. His more liberal sisters are fascinated by Lucie's history. Only Mrs. Reinertson does not censor her. To Mrs. Reinertson, Lucie is a 'new woman' who claims the right to the same sexual history as her husband. Since all men are sexually active, it is only fair that women be sexually active too. Her sister is more censorious. Sensing Knut's interest in Lucie, Henny creates an imaginary sexual history for herself, one that mirrors Lucie's. The libertine Knut collapses in tears of joy when he discovers it is only a fiction. Everybody projects their own meaning onto Lucie and the woman she used to be. Significantly, all the people in the book call her by a different name. To her old friend Nilsa from Tivoli she is 'Luciekins,' to Olsen her former lover she is 'Lucia' or 'Lussia,' to the Reinertsons she's the 'Tivoli-wife.' Even for the most liberal members of society, Lucie is as marked as Hester Prynne in *The Scarlet Letter.* In spite of all Lucie's efforts to escape it, Lucie's past sticks to her like the dirt that besmirches her curtains, the dust that won't rub off her fine furniture. It is a stain that exists not only in society's eyes but also in her own. She is aware of the great gulf that separates her from the other women in her society and she cannot free her mind from the woman she used to be. When she thinks about her past she shies away from descriptive words: 'She was just as good as Theodor and didn't need to be ashamed because she had been like *that*.' 'She means *me*, a woman who has been... she knows about it and just the same...' It is as if the words themselves are dirty to Lucie. She has learned the middle class values of society too well not to judge herself. The rigour of those judgments can be seen in the aftermath of the evening Lucie spends at Nilsa's. In the old Tivoli milieu, she reverts to the laughing, sensuous, active girl she once was. But after an evening basking in Nilsa and Olsen's love and acceptance, she instantly rejects her old friends when she sees her husband on the street. The Lucie who lives in her husband's world is ashamed of the warmth and spontaneity of the past.

Living with her husband on Incognitogaten, her feelings and motives in disguise, Lucie is not the only character who seeks to escape the constrictions of life through role-playing. Images of the theatre – costumes, masquerades, dances, and hypnotic performances – figure prominently in the novel. At the Mørks' party, the host urges his guests to '*act* your parts to your heart's content'. The masked party guests comply, and so do other characters in the novel. The aura of theatre is reinforced by Skram's chapter headings, most of which precisely locate the scenes that follow in time and space: 'In the Professor's Quarter,' 'At the Mørks,' 'During the Night.' The headings are like set descriptions, and they emphasise the performance aspects of the novel. As in a play, the novel proceeds in scenes and acts. Each act of the novel is organised around Amalie Skram's familiar pattern of escape and return.

Lucie's rebellions

Like many of Amalie Skram's heroines, Lucie looks for wider spaces, more promising spheres for action. Repeatedly Lucie rebels against the constraints of her surroundings and escapes into a green world of greater freedom and possibility. There are small escapes and large ones: marriage to Gerner, a visit to Nilsa, dancing and masquerades at the Reinertsons', a trip to Malmø, a hypnotic trance. Each escape ends in a punishing return. Chapter III runs through the whole process in one chapter: Lucie offends Theodor by laughing and drinking toasts with their friend Mørk; Theodor criticises the way she plays her role; Lucie cries and begs forgiveness. Chapters IV-VII show a more dramatic series of escapes, followed by the inevitable return: A small rebellion against Theodor's instruction leads Lucie into a cascade of escapes, first to Mrs. Reinertson's house, then to a recreation of her past at Nilsa's, and finally to a tipsy spree, complete with her old Tivoli costumes in front of the mirror. But after two days of silence from her husband, Lucie can bear no more and begs forgiveness. Throughout the novel, the pattern is repeated: escape is followed by a painful return. In her progress from one punishing episode to the next, Lucie's spirit is dampened but not extinguished. As her husband observes, she's like a spring that 'jumps back whenever you push it down'.

Outside the boundaries of marriage as well as within it Lucie experiences a series of violations, first of body and then spirit. When she meets Lieutenant Knut Reinertson she is dazzled by the handsome young man who appears to be an image of gentility. She meets him at a masquerade party, his military uniform concealed by the costume of a monk. Lieutenant 'Lionheart's' character is as deceptive as his clothing. Beguiled by his gentlemanly manners, Lucie blissfully dances off in the lieutenant's arms, ignoring her husband's discomfort. Walking home after the party, she rejects Gerner's accusations of impropriety and runs into the night. The fence Lucie climbs over this time is literal rather than social. Far beyond the civilised streets of the town, Lucie lies down to rest in a field, her mind filled with dreams of the lieutenant. Again she has a punishing encounter with male will – a physical one this time. She is raped by a passing vagrant, a dirty, violent exemplar of male lust. The experience is a violent echo of her transgression and punishment earlier that evening. Lucie returns home bruised and battered – forcibly reminded of her lower class origins.

Lucie's escape to Malmø is intended as a simple night away from the claustrophobic spaces of her marriage. But the short boat trip to the island opens several new worlds for her. On Malmø she listens to the talk of educated women, and learns there are other ways to regard her past than the ones she has known. For a short time she can escape from her own sense of contamination. Meeting the lieutenant again simply deepens his allure for her. An expert in ingratiating games, the lieutenant is a new type for Lucie. His power, like hers, lies in his youth and beauty. She believes that his elegant manners are a sign of his gentility. She does not see that he is a careless flirt who toys with women for his own amusement. A lower-class woman with a past,

Lucie is fair game in his society. Once he is sure Lucie will yield to him he has no further interest in her. His impact on Lucie is made manifest in the scene at Malmø in which he hypnotises her. A parlour game to him, hypnosis is viewed as morally questionable by his aunt and Henny, who see the sexual appropriation implicit in it. Henny's resistance to hypnosis contrasts with Lucie's eager susceptibility. Lucie quickly falls into a hypnotic trance and yields her mind and body to the lieutenant's control. Like a Pygmalion in reverse, the lieutenant turns a living body into an object with rigid limbs and a stony face. After making Lucie sit and stand at his command, he orders her to come to his apartment the following week. Improbably, Knut proposes marriage shortly afterwards to Henny. Skram wants us to see the difference between these relationships. When Knut proposes marriage, Henny stages a little drama for him. She casts herself as a woman with a past, and tells him she had lovers in Paris. She puts herself outside the boundaries of their middle class milieu and watches what he does. When he says he wants to marry her anyway, that he will always be faithful, Henny joyfully accepts him. Presumably their marriage will be different to Lucie and Gerner's, because each accepts the other for what they are. Neither will enter the marriage with mistaken ideas about the other, neither will try to recreate the other. Together they will make a place where equals meet.

Lucie's conversion

Images of defilement spread in the last section of Skram's book. Lucie has experienced male lust, even male assault, but being treated as inconsequential is something new. Ensnared in the lieutenant's seductive games and unceremoniously dumped when he wins Henny for his wife, Lucie covers her shame by creating a new role for herself. This time it does not come from the romantic pages of a novel, or from the risqué entertainments of Tivoli. She will take charge of her own transformation this time, and undergo a religious conversion. She will become God's handmaiden, dedicating herself to her personal salvation. She chooses the Free Church rather than the State Church embodied in Pastor Brandt. Enraptured by this new identity, she leaves the house only to hear her minister's sermons. She dedicates herself to the Bible and to her conversion, praying that God will make her clean again. The sign will be the baby born without the birthmark of the man who raped her.

Gerner succeeds in his efforts to transform Lucie, but instead of making a respectable bourgeois housewife, he takes a living, breathing woman and turns her to stone. Once quick to laugh and dance, Lucie becomes passive, immobile, silent. She loses her humanity, consumed from within by the baby growing inside her, furious with all men, unable to see the transformations in Gerner's character, finally unable to even accept her innocent son, born with the fearful birthmark. In the harrowing childbirth scene, Lucie has laboured to deliver the proof that God loves her. But even surrendering herself to the Lord has failed to accomplish its purpose. She looks back at her life and sees nothing but false dreams and sexual exploitation. Marriage, rape, seduction, betrayal, pregnancy, childbirth – all of these landmarks in Lucie's development carry the same message: she has been occupied in mind and body by male expectations and desires, and that occupation has destroyed her. The loving, high-spirited girl ends as something less than human, and her death from puerperal fever is simply the final step in her downward progression. On her deathbed, embittered and delirious, there is one last flare-up of Lucie's will. She hallucinates a funeral carriage with only the people she chooses allowed inside: Nilsa, Mrs. Reinertson and Knut. With all their limitations and failures, each one has defended or acknowledged Lucie's right to exist as a sexual being. Only her husband has tried to obliterate this part of her nature. She refuses to let him ride in the carriage. Somewhere in her consciousness the drive toward freedom still has flickering life.

Where do Amalie Skram's sympathies lie in this strange and powerful novel? Her portrayal of Lucie's decline piles horror upon horror. Throughout the novel Lucie has struggled valiantly to improve herself, and her best has never been enough. Skram vividly portrays Lucie's despair and anger. But there are two victims in the Gerner marriage. Both are presented with all their contradictions. Skram mercilessly exposes Gerner's arrogance and pride, but she also shows his suffering. In spite of his frustration and misery, Gerner's love for his wife endures. He tenderly cares for Lucie during her difficult pregnancy and accepts her abuse without recrimination. As Lucie is dying, he thinks back on their life together and absolves himself from blame. He believes he has been an honourable husband, who has striven to make their marriage succeed. But if there is blindness in his final assessment, there is also a new humility. Accepting his own impotence, he is a chastened figure. At the end of the novel, Gerner is left with Lucie's baby, born with a birthmark, a baby not his blood but his hope for the future, a second chance to love and accept human imperfections.

Katherine Hanson
Judith Messick

Notes

i. For a perceptive discussion of *Lucie* and its relationship to other of Skram's marriage novels, see Irene Englestad's important book: *Sammenbrudd og Gjennombrudd*, (1984: Oslo, Pax Forlag A/S).

ii. Probably inspired by the Canon of Toledo in *Don Quixote*, Charlotte Lennox created the figure of the learned Doctor for her novel *The Female Quixote; or The Adventures of Arabella, (1752)*. In all of his more modern incarnations the learned Doctor is a male authority figure who, with varying degrees of success, tries to mould the young heroine into an acceptable member of society.

iii. Englestad notes the many instances in the book in which washing or ritual cleansing figure prominently.

iv. Shaw's *Pygmalion* was published almost two decades later than *Lucie* in 1913. Quotes are from the Penguin edition.

v. 'Stanzas from the Grande Chartreuse,' 85-86.